Intentions

Barbara Winkes

ISBN: 978-1-0693045-2-0

Cover art © May Dawney Designs

Created with Atticus

For D.

Chapter One

L ife was good. Nothing to worry about. With a sharp focus, Jordan took aim at the target and pulled the trigger, three times, four, five, hitting the mark each time. She had needed the practice, and it was good to see she hadn't lost her touch. That was all there was to her visit to the shooting range. It had nothing to do with the appearance of Darby's lawyer, or the news he'd brought.

Or the letter.

Jordan wasn't interested in what Darby had to say to her. Based on her experience, she could tell without reading the letter that he'd try to get under her skin one more time, make her doubt herself. He wouldn't succeed.

She was letting go of the house he'd sold her. The case was long closed, and the letter didn't contain information to magically solve others, she was certain. Darby had nothing to give to her, because he knew she wouldn't offer him anything in return.

Truth be told, she was angry. Not at his last attempt at manipulating her—Jordan wasn't surprised at that. He was supposed to spend the rest of his life behind bars, years and decades to come, but the end of that time was coming sooner than they'd all expected. Too easy on him, after the terror he'd inflicted on his victims. Too quick.

Another round. Jordan suppressed a sigh. Practice, right. She didn't need a shrink to tell her that with the parameters having changed once again, she needed to feel in control—the last step to closure. She didn't know if he had weeks or months. She didn't want to know.

She'd met with a realtor named Andrea Cox earlier today to discuss the sale of her house. The woman was also in charge of finding Jordan and Ellie a new home. She was moving on.

Darby couldn't go anywhere. There was solace in that, for her, for the other survivors, the victims' loved ones.

Time to go home.

She had some cleaning up to do. The realtor had assured her that the house was in good shape and almost ready for an open house. She had to consult with Ellie regarding dates for viewings of their own. She had barely seen her this week as Ellie was working nights at the moment.

She was also waiting for the test results of the detective's exam she'd taken.

Jordan was excited for her, though she had no doubt Ellie had aced the exam, because she'd tackled it like everything else in life. Frankly, she was more focused on the future living arrangements, mostly thrilled about the prospect, a small part of her still terrified. Those were voices of the past, though, her former self. Just because she'd messed up once—okay, a few times—it didn't mean she'd to it again.

This was different. Ellie was different.

"That was pretty impressive." Back at the front door, she turned around at the sound of a familiar voice.

"I didn't know you were here," she said, surprised.

Derek Henderson, her partner, shrugged. "Nothing better to do on a Friday evening, I guess. What's your excuse?"

That didn't sound good. Jordan wasn't sure Ellie had managed to talk to Kate yet, Derek's girlfriend with whom she was sharing an apartment at the moment.

"Ellie is working nights. I'm stalling getting my house cleaned up. Want to have dinner?"

"Sure, why not? There's this new burger joint on Madison. Max's?"

"I've heard about it. Sounds good. I'll meet you there."

The moment she sat in her car, Jordan wondered if she might regret her offer. There were a few elephants in the room to maneuver around, and they mostly had to do with Kate.

Jordan and Ellie had decided that it was the right time for the two of them to move in together, but Ellie also wanted to give Kate a fair warning. Their community had been shaken by the death of a fellow officer who had been Kate's fiancé. In the aftermath, Kate and Derek had gotten close, and she and Ellie had become roommates. Recently, Kate made the decision to leave the force. More major changes were coming, and she wasn't sure if tonight was the right time to discuss them all.

A couple of red lights slowed her down, so when she arrived, Derek had already ordered a beer. The waitress brought it before she could consider her own choice.

"That looks good. I'll go with the same," Jordan told her, then she and Derek both went back to studying the menu.

"Kate broke up with me."

The statement came without warning, and it took her a moment to react properly.

"Damn. I'm so sorry." Jordan laid down the menu.

"Don't get me wrong," he added quickly. "I wasn't going to complain to you. I just wanted to tell you before it goes around, and I don't know if she talked to Ellie."

"I didn't know, I swear. I'm really—"

"Yeah, thanks. We can move on to something else now."

For Jordan, that wasn't going quite as quick. There were so many implications in this, Kate being apparently hell-bent on ending her career as a cop, now her relationship with Derek, what would that mean for Jordan and Ellie's plans? She chided herself for being selfish. The truth was Kate was still grieving. She probably needed to feel in control as well, even though it was questionable whether all those breaks would help. Then again, Jordan could only speak for herself. The recent challenges, some of them traumatic, had made her priorities even clearer—being a cop, being with Ellie.

"Sure. Ellie should have her results any day now."

They'd spent a lot of time together lately, her and Derek, Ellie, and Kate. Those changes would take some time to get used to for all of them.

"She's not worried? She's been getting ready for this from the first day out of the academy."

"I'm not worried. She's...cautious," Jordan phrased her words carefully, unable to keep the smile off her face. She was happy these days, proud of the woman she loved...maybe she wasn't the best company for Derek tonight.

"So, you read the letter Donovan gave you? Anything new, or was it the same old crap you expected?"

"No, I didn't read it, for exactly that reason. I already knew it would be the same old crap." She didn't know what to make of his expression. "Anyway, you saw me throw it out after he left. I'm good, I swear. I think Darby gets an easy way out, but there's nothing anyone can do about it now."

"Ellie took it. She probably thinks you might change your mind at some point, so you'll still have the chance."

"Okay. I see."

"Don't be mad at her. She means well."

"I have no doubt. Wow. This is...unexpected." If she was honest, Jordan would have liked not to know, because she was sure Ellie wouldn't bring up the subject unless Jordan did—so, preferably, never. "I'm not going to be mad, come on, we're adults. Why are you telling me this now?"

He shrugged. "That's actually a good question. I thought you should know. Maybe I'm a bit jealous of people who have a handle on their relationships. I'm sorry."

"That's okay. I'm sure Kate just needs more time—and your assessment is debatable...but yeah, things are finally good. That's the reason why I don't bother with Darby's games."

"You're not curious at all?"

"No. I already know all there is to him." Derek stayed silent at that. "He's not going to give up more victims. Did he kill more than we know about? Maybe, but he knows he's not getting anything from us. This will be the end of it. I don't mind if Ellie wants to know what's in the letter, if she gets some closure from it, but I don't need that."

"However you want to handle it. You know I'll have your back."

"Thank you. Now that we've got that out of the way, how about the weather now?"

They both laughed, intent on postponing any dire subjects for a little while longer.

Chapter Two

Ellie had made several half-hearted attempts at bringing up the living arrangements earlier during roll call, but then Kate was assigned with Casey Lyons, and she hadn't seen her since. She had wanted to talk some more about Kate's career plans as well, but Kate informed her that she'd already turned in her resignation. She'd be gone by the end of the month. She didn't share any other plans.

Ellie wanted to be a friend to her. She also needed to take some chances. In the past few days, she'd been focusing on the test before anything else, but now that it was done, it was time.

No more stalling. After tonight's shift, she had to find Kate and talk to her.

The future was looking bright.

Even though Jordan had only mentioned it offhandedly once, there was the chance that a colleague of hers, Detective Waters, might retire soon, and that would mean an opening in Homicide. This had always been Ellie's goal, right from the start, and it seemed within reach. So was finally sharing a home with Jordan. She couldn't have been happier.

Okay, there was the letter still burning a hole in her pocket, but she'd try her best not to make too much of it. If Jordan ever mentioned being curious about it...she could offer. If not, they never had to mention it again.

She was distracted from her various planning when she saw a person on the sidewalk waving to her, obviously trying to catch her attention.

"Officer! We need some help here!"

Ellie parked the car and got out, joining the small group, two women and a man, all in their late forties to early fifties.

"What happened? Do you need an ambulance?"

One of the women shook her head, exasperated. "I don't think so, but if you can get him to stop yelling, that would be great. We were having guests over, and that's not the entertainment we were looking for."

Ellie quickly understood what she was looking at when the man in question, a few feet away, started shouting again.

"I hate the bitch! She was a bad mother to you. Hate her!"

The obviously drunk individual was in his late twenties maybe, wearing jeans and a tank top. He was walking farther down the street, but then made a sharp turn, coming back.

"We were discussing whether to call the police," the other woman said, "but then we saw you. Maybe you could just talk to him?"

"Bitch!" the man yelled. Ellie saw he was carrying a cat on his shoulder that, unlike the neighbors, seemed pretty much used to his antics. It looked fairly comfortable.

"Of course. Sir. Could I talk to you for a moment?" she asked, walking towards him. He made a step, stumbled slightly, but managed to stay upright and hold on to the cat. "Are you okay?"

"Bitch," he said again, obviously having trouble focusing. "Left me. She's not going to get the cat. Did the bitch call you?"

Ellie winced. Aside from screaming every single word, the man had obviously been drinking all night—she could smell it on his breath.

"No, but the people on this street have had quite enough of your yelling. Why don't you go home and get some sleep?"

"Why don't you LEAVE ME ALONE?"

It's the full moon, Ellie thought, suppressing the impulse to shake her head. Just this one more night shift, and she could spend some time at Jordan's, sleep, breakfast, sex. She could do one more night, especially since she'd probably know the test results next week. A whole new life would begin soon.

"I'm sorry, sir, but you're bothering the neighbors. If you could just keep it down..."

It would have been too much to ask for.

He pushed her—not hard, he didn't have the coordination left to do that—and then ran. Stumbled, was more like it, while the cat was still comfortably curled up on his shoulder.

"Hey! Stop!"

Of course, he didn't. Ellie caught up with him just before he was about to walk right into traffic.

"Fuck you," he spat at her, teetering on his feet before he passed out. The cat saved itself with a quick jump and then hurried back in the direction the man had come from.

Ellie kneeled beside him to check for his pulse and then got out her phone.

"I guess we need that ambulance after all," she said to no one. Her call was almost drowned out by a driver revving up his engine, mistaking the street for a racetrack.

That kind of night.

Thank God the new life was just around the corner.

When Jordan moved into the house, she had been in a hurry to get out of the apartment she'd then shared with Bethany. She'd taken her personal belongings and left most of the furniture. She realized that it would be the same when she left her current home. Maybe the new owner would be willing to factor some of it into the price of the house.

Jordan went to her bedroom, opened closets, and closed them again. A well-organized household. She'd always made sure that everything was in place in case she had to leave abruptly, and it had served her—confirmation or self-fulfilling prophecy?

It was time for something permanent. She wasn't living with a couple of unfit parents or a girlfriend she didn't know how to leave. This was her choice.

Still, she'd have to talk to Ellie about the letter, *thank you, but no, I don't care what's in it.*

She hadn't told anyone, because she didn't want her friends and family to think she considered this house a mistake in the first place—it had been a good idea at the time—now, she couldn't wait to leave.

<hr />

Ellie had hardly ever been so happy to leave the station. She envisioned a hot shower and maybe a couple of hours of sleep at Jordan's after finally figuring out with the help of various services how to best deal with Yelling Man. He had come to before the ambulance arrived and hadn't slowed down since.

"Bitch stole my cat! Arrest her!" was one of the nicer things he'd hurled at Ellie.

He couldn't go home, because he claimed his ex, the cat's "mom" had locked him out. Finally, they came to an agreement that he would stay at the station overnight to sober up, and that there would be a follow-up with the hospital to determine if he was a threat to anyone, including himself.

The address he'd named was indeed close to the street where neighbors had asked Ellie to talk to him, and when she stepped onto the small porch of the house, a soft meow made her turn around.

"You're home, aren't you?" she said, reaching out to pet the tabby cat, then picked it up at the same time the woman opened the door.

"Oh, Minnie, you're back! Thank you so much, Officer. Wait. You're not here because of Minnie." She sighed heavily. "It's Kevin, right? He went on a binge again."

"Your ex-boyfriend?" Ellie asked, and the woman's eyes widened.

"He told you that? I gave him soup once. He really liked Minnie."

Ellie had a suspicion, which after a few minutes' worth of conversation was confirmed. Kevin, who lived by himself in an apartment down the street, was an example for how people would fall through the cracks of society, when at the same time, their behavior was indulged and never analyzed all the way to the roots. For sure, he had his problems. He might or might not become dangerous at some point to a female neighbor who'd once been nice to him, because he felt entitled, to her affection and maybe more.

Ellie took out a card and wrote her cell phone number on the bottom.

"He's probably going to be okay once he sobers up, but if you need anything, please call."

She didn't think she'd ever hear from her again, but it was the least she could do.

Half an hour later, she parked in front of Jordan's house and let herself in, heading straight to the shower, assuming that Jordan was still asleep.

Clad in only a towel, she walked into the bedroom and got underneath the sheets with her, deciding that breakfast could wait a little while longer.

"Hey," Jordan murmured, reaching for her. "You want breakfast in bed?"

"Just bed will be okay for a while.

She was asleep within minutes, only later woken by the scent of coffee and bacon. Ellie got dressed in her own panties and Jordan's shirt and combed her hands through her hair. Jordan acknowledged her appearance with an amused smile.

"Long night?"

"Oh yeah. Sometimes it makes you wonder if we can ever do enough for people. It seems like everyone's only thinking about what happens after the fact, never about prevention."

"It feels like that sometimes," Jordan said, but didn't deepen the subject.

"It does." Ellie poured herself a cup of coffee and sat down at the table, gazing out of the window. The view of the trees and mountains in the distance was nice, but not nice enough to overlook the connection to Darby with this property. They had evaded the subject of him successfully for some time now, but the recent past had brought triggers, like the last case that led not only to a woman-hating cult being shut down, but a serial murderer brought to justice. Joseph's trial would begin soon.

She wondered how Ariel was doing. The young girl had grown up in the cult and was now a material witness. They had promised to keep in touch, but it would be easier after her testimony. They didn't want anyone to allege they might be influencing her—too much depended on her, and Ariel knew that. The last time they'd talked, Ariel had moved from her temporary placement into a group home for young teens.

"I know you have the letter," Jordan said, startling Ellie out of her thoughts. Her tone was light, non accusatory. Still, Ellie felt the need to explain herself.

"I didn't read it. I wanted to...give you the chance in case you change your mind."

Jordan shook her head. "I'm not going to."

"I'm sorry."

"It's okay." Jordan turned off the stove and put some bacon and eggs on Ellie's plate, then her own. "You can read it if you want. I don't mind or care. I don't want anything to do with it."

"Derek told you?"

"Come on. Eat. It's fine. Let's forget about it." There was the slightest edge to her tone.

"Okay. How did it go with the realtor?" Ellie wasn't sure how she felt about Jordan giving her permission to read what Darby had written to her. Maybe they were all overestimating him, though there was no denying he had been fixating on her. There was no telling what was in it until one of them actually read it.

"She says we could do an open house in a couple of weeks—have you talked to Kate yet?"

Ellie had been unsuccessful trying to find her at the end of her shift, and frankly, she'd been too tired.

"Not yet. After this weekend, I swear."

"I know you've been busy, but this is kind of important. I might be homeless soon."

"That's ridiculous, you won't be homeless! You can always stay with me until we find—" Ellie stopped midway in her explanation when she realized Jordan was yanking her chain. "That's not fair. You've been up longer than I have."

"Sorry about that. However, Derek told me they broke up."

"Oh no. That's going to make me sound like a bitch. A happy, crazy in love bitch, but nonetheless." Ellie sighed. "I know it's selfish, but I wish we could have this time to figure it all out without the drama all around. I can't even blame her. I sure have made some rash decisions after something bad happened...Not you," she added quickly. "Don't even go there. When I first saw you, I wanted your life, and I wanted you."

"Oh, wow," Jordan said, clearly self-conscious.

"It's true. I'm worried Kate will regret all of this. She's not all that sure what she's going to do instead of being a cop—and Derek's a good guy. So, this is really none of my business, but I have to tell her. I guess I'll see if I catch her later."

"Yes, but finish your breakfast first."

Jordan had barely finished the words when Ellie's cell phone rang from somewhere in the bedroom. By the time she found it, the ring tone had stopped, and there was a text message from Kate.

"Hey, E. I took the rest of the vacation days I had left, and I'm going to hide out at my grandparents for a bit. Don't worry, I'll cover my part of the rent. I just need to get away from it all. Good luck, Kate."

Ellie called her number, glad Kate picked up right away. "What's going on? Are you okay?"

Kate laughed wistfully. "I think so. I haven't done anything spontaneous like this in more than a decade, so I can't say for sure, but...I'll be okay. Don't worry."

"Jordan and I are looking for a place together," Ellie blurted out. "Oh my God, I wanted to find such a better moment to tell you. When are you leaving?"

"Cab's here now, so I can't talk much longer. It's okay, Ellie. Don't think I haven't seen this coming. I'm happy for you."

Was this too easy?

"Keep in touch, okay? I really hope everything works out for you."

"You too. You haven't gotten your results yet?"

"It's Saturday, so...I'll let you know. Have a good trip."

When she ended the call, she saw Jordan standing in the doorway and walked right into her embrace. Both of them were tempted by the unmade bed, the idea of shutting out the world for a little while longer—because whenever something new, better, began, something else had to end. They'd both had their share of that.

※

Ellie had planned to go back to her apartment on Sunday night, but Jordan didn't have to work hard to convince her to stay, even if it meant they had to get up early on Monday morning.

Ellie wanted to check a few things before work, but when she let herself in, she wondered if there was really anything pressing. The place felt too empty and big now, reminding her of her previous apartment she had first shared with Rhonda, and then rented by herself. Her ex hadn't been as gracious as Kate, leaving Ellie hanging with the rent or space she didn't need. Then she'd met Jordan. And Jordan bought a house. Complicated, adult affairs...She couldn't wait for the day when they'd have everything sorted out and could start their lives together.

She went to her bedroom where she'd put the letter into a desk drawer and took it out again. Closure. Endings. Beginnings.

Stalling, Ellie put it aside and turned on her laptop instead to check her emails.

What she saw distracted her for a moment from the other task at hand. When had she last checked...Of course. Before her shift. She hadn't expected the email to come on a weekend, but...

There it was.

Truth be told, at the moment, she almost dreaded opening it as much as reading Darby's words. What if she had been fooling herself all this time? What if she didn't make it?

That wasn't possible. She had been well prepared. She had known the answers.

Ellie clicked on the mail, and then her eyes welled up when the content was exactly what she had hoped for. How could she have had any doubts? She hadn't lied to Jordan the other morning—this was what she had always wanted, and she was much closer to realizing that goal. There might not be an opening in Homicide right now, but she could try out for a department a bit further away. In fact, it might be good for her and Jordan if they didn't work so closely together, at least for a while. Their other plans would definitely make up for the time they couldn't see each other at work.

After everything that had happened in the past few months, she knew Jordan felt protective of her, and the same was true vice versa, but in their respective careers, they had to give each other the necessary space.

Finally, she took a deep breath and picked up the letter, to get this over with too. She'd have to write a text to Kate and tell her the news. Call Jordan. The rest of their friends could wait until tomorrow.

Ellie removed the single sheet of paper from the envelope and started to read.

My Dear Jordan...

Chapter Three

*M*y Dear Jordan,

    As you probably already know, I am dying. Obviously, that's not your fault, but there's no denying you made mistakes. All of our actions have consequences. You stopped me from fulfilling my mission, but since I liked you the best of all my subjects, I decided to give you a word of warning.

    It saddens me that I won't be the one to teach you, but we can't always get what we want, can we? It's out of my hands now. I hope that when the time comes, you'll be ready.

    We shall meet again on the other side.

    Yours sincerely,

    J.D.

When Ellie stood on her doorstep less than half an hour after going to her apartment, Jordan knew right away that she didn't have good news. There was no way she could have failed the test, that, Jordan knew with certainty.

"This must be really important if you couldn't wait to tell me at work."

"I passed the exam. They emailed this weekend."

"That's great! I mean I knew you would. Aren't you happy?" Perhaps Ellie was still in the grip of the past weeks' stress, the work schedule, studying, preparing for the test. That was an explanation as good as any, was it?

"I am. I swear…but I think we cannot ignore this," Ellie said somberly.

Jordan recognized the folded piece of paper Ellie had taken out of her purse, right away. "No. Whatever it is, forget about it."

"We need to take it to Lieutenant Carroll. At the very least, he needs to be aware of it."

"Unless there are specific threats, I don't think—" Jordan resisted the urge to simply walk away from the conversation, but barely. She knew Ellie had only her best interests at heart, but she wished she'd let it go. Darby's days were counted. He could threaten her all he wanted to. It wouldn't change anything—for him, for her. They had something to celebrate. The past had to stay in the past.

"They are a bit vague, but yes, there are threats."

Ellie leaned forward, embracing her, making it impossible for Jordan to distance herself.

"I'm sorry. I'd never bother you with this if I didn't think it meant something."

It was silly, really. Words on paper couldn't hurt her. *He* couldn't.

"I need to go to work," she said, her resistance faltering.

"I know. I can drive, and you read it on the way."

Apparently, she had no choice in the matter—and when had she ever been able to say no to Ellie?

Less than five minutes later, Jordan tossed the paper onto the dashboard, mulling the words over, fairly surprised. She didn't know what she'd expected, perhaps an evil spell rising from the words? This was pure megalomaniac Darby, thinking she'd care what he thought, hoping to get a rise out of her. She wasn't going to see him and press him on the vague hints as to events in the future. Jordan was also certain that Lieutenant Carroll wouldn't want to waste manpower on that subject.

Ellie waited patiently.

"Nothing will come out of this. With him, it's too easy to jump to conclusions, and he knows it. We got it wrong the other time, remember?" she asked softly. Of course, Ellie remembered what happened when they'd thought Darby was in contact with her stalker. The truth had been even closer.

"Better to be safe than sorry, right?"

Jordan had to admit that the lieutenant would probably want to be in the know about Darby's last-ditch efforts. She sighed.

Then, so be it.

"All right."

⌑

"Good thinking, Harding. You bet I want to know about this."

Jordan tried not to wince, as the lieutenant turned his gaze on her. Whatever it was, reproach or sympathy, she wasn't in the mood for either on this Monday morning.

"If that's all…" she started.

"We'll check in with the warden about any recent contacts. We won't leave anything to chance where that son of a bitch is concerned."

"Thanks," Jordan mumbled, placing her hand on Ellie's shoulder to remind her it was time to go.

"Just a minute, Detective Carpenter."

"Sure."

Ellie gave Lieutenant Carroll a polite smile and left.

"Sir, I am really sorry," Jordan said after Ellie had closed the door behind her. "I know this is nothing."

He shook his head, looking exasperated. "Did you not hear what I said? This might be nothing, if that's the case, great. In case Darby is fantasizing about orchestrating some great finale from behind bars, we should all be aware of it, don't you think?"

"He's bluffing."

"Do you know that for certain?"

"I think I know him better than most people," she said, feeling a headache build behind her temples. Rehashing this subject once again, with Lieutenant Carroll no less, would do that.

"Yes, I am aware. And there's something else you should remember: None of what happened, was your fault. Judy Lawrence is alive because of you. Let's make sure he doesn't get anything out of this."

Jordan was sure that Darby was already enjoying himself at the thought of anyone taking the letter seriously. For the sake of ending the conversation, she relented.

"I appreciate that, sir. Can I go now?"

"Of course."

She had intended to sneak into the break room for a fresh coffee when she realized a small group had gathered, with Ellie at the center of it. Jordan thought guiltily that this day shouldn't be about her. She went and got herself a coffee, then joined the group. Ellie gave her an apologetic smile.

Everything's fine. We're fine. At least, that's what Jordan hoped to convey.

"Well, congratulations, Detective Harding," she said, tapping her cup lightly against Ellie's. The uniformed officers with her cheered.

"Don't party too hard," Jordan advised, amused. "It's only Monday morning."

20

They were right on track. Less than a couple of weeks later, Ellie had to restrain the impulse to bounce down the stairs of the 12th precinct. This hadn't been her first choice, obviously, and the job would come with a long commute too—then again, she and Jordan hadn't yet made a choice regarding a house, so that wasn't anything to worry about now. Perhaps it wasn't such a bad idea that they wouldn't work in the same unit right away. Truth be told, as confident as Ellie was about her own skills and résumé, she still felt a tad intimidated sometimes watching the detectives in her own precinct at work. She knew it mostly stemmed from the time when she'd hung out with her friends at the *Code 7*, watching their table with an interest that went far beyond the professional. Now, she had a place at the table, and not just for her relationship with Jordan.

She had earned that place. Ellie was fairly certain that the interview had gone well. The lieutenant of the other department's Homicide unit knew Sergeant Bristol and their precinct. Ellie had worked on the periphery of several high-profile cases. This was her time. The position had to be filled soon because another detective was going on maternity leave. By the time she returned, perhaps there would be a place for Ellie in a Homicide unit closer to home.

It was a big relief as well that according to the prison staff, Darby was having his usual delusions of grandeur. The only visitors came from the law firm representing him. There was no other interaction with the outside otherwise. He got some fan mail, but that only went one way.

She didn't regret bringing the letter to Lieutenant Carroll's attention.

Better to be safe than sorry.

She started the car and turned on the radio. It was going to be a good day.

Ellie was still waiting to hear back about the interview when the realtor called them to make an appointment for another viewing. It was thrilling that all of this was happening at the same time, big, life-changing decisions to be made all in one year. She couldn't wait.

The way to the house where she was meeting Jordan and their realtor after work took her an extra twenty minutes due to a detour. What you wished for most wasn't always the most practical, and she regretted chiding Jordan often for that half hour commute she'd accepted when buying the house.

But like everything else, they'd figure it out.

Jordan and the realtor, Andrea Cox, were waiting for her in the parking lot.

"I'm sorry," she said. "Construction sites are popping on every other street."

"How did it go?" Jordan asked while Cox unlocked the door of the two-story building for them.

"Fine, I think. It'll take some time to get there, but I'm excited."

"I'm excited for you." Jordan kissed her quickly, and they walked into the elegant living/dining space.

"I like the fireplace," Ellie said. "This is a nice neighborhood. I didn't know all of it was in our budget."

Andrea looked apologetic. "It's not exactly, but I really wanted you to see this. It's been on the market for a bit, so there's more than likely room to negotiate."

"Okay, let's take a look."

No more rash decisions. No more thinking anything could be too good to be true.

As much as they'd both liked the house, Jordan and Ellie had agreed that they needed to see more places that fit their budget better. In a perfect world, Ellie's promotion would come through right away, but they both knew they couldn't rely on that. That caution was warranted, Jordan realized when Ellie called her with the news that morning. She had just stepped out of the car at the crime scene she and Derek had been called to.

"I didn't get it. I don't understand this, after all this gushing about Bristol and our precinct." Ellie's disappointment rang clearly. Jordan was disappointed, too, for her.

"Oh, baby, I'm sorry. I can't talk right now, but I'll see you later. There will be something else."

"Yeah, sure. I need to go back, too. Bye."

"Bye."

Jordan hated having to hang up on Ellie at this moment, but there wasn't much of an alternative as she was standing over the dead body of a college student who had been found behind a dumpster. He had his wallet with him, but there were no credit cards or money in it, only his college ID. It was a rather well-known fact that crime was high in this neighborhood, which prompted the question: What had Colin Buck been doing here, quite far away from campus?

Derek stood a few feet away with the woman who had found him. She was running the small corner store in a building that looked like it might not last much longer.

"I'm used to hearing shots every once in a while," she said, "but this is new."

There were two visible gunshot wounds on the dead man's body. As to why he'd been killed, she could think of several possibilities. Drugs were one of them. Someone might have even gone through his pockets after he was killed.

"Anything unusual in the past few days?" Jordan asked. "A car, or people you didn't recognize?"

The woman shrugged. "I don't know everybody who lives around here, but there have been some guys hanging around, waiting for I don't know what. Not as clean cut as him, but I am sure they were up to nothing good. I chased them away. If they're doing drugs around here, it's not good for business. People are scared as it is."

"Do you have any names?"

"What do you think? They didn't volunteer."

"That's okay. If you could describe them to us?"

"Nothing much I can tell you. They were wearing jeans, baseball caps...wait, one of them was wearing a Jersey with the number six on it. Red, I think."

"Okay, that's good, thank you." Jordan turned around, shielding her eyes against the sun as she looked up one of those grey depressing blocks that surrounded them. The street was empty. It was unlikely that they'd find a witness here. Finding that group of men hanging around might help.

She remembered that one of her former CI's, Darla Pierson, had lived around here. She'd ask her some questions. Meanwhile, they'd have to visit Buck's school to find out more—and unfortunately, notify his family.

⁂

The college's dean confirmed that Colin Buck had enrolled four years ago. He would have graduated this year.

"There was never any trouble," the dean, a woman in her late fifties, said. "Not that we have a lot here, but his name never came up. Excellent grades. He's from Tacoma. This is terrible," she added with a sigh. "I suppose you'll have to notify the parents. I'll have to talk to them too. How very sad."

"We'd like to see his dorm room," Derek said, and she nodded.

"Of course. Come with me."

Curious looks followed them as they walked across the campus to the dorms, and into the building.

Buck's room was fairly typical, textbooks, some sports memorabilia, and a jacket over a chair, a half-empty bottle of coke on the desk. Jordan lifted it with a gloved hand, but it didn't smell like anything else. The laptop was going straight to the lab. No cell phone had been found with Colin Buck, and it didn't look like there was one in here. She was opening drawers when the roommate came in.

"Whoa, what happened? Is Colin in trouble?"

"Why do you think that?" Derek asked sternly, and the student blushed.

"You're the police, right? You wouldn't be going through his stuff if...Is he okay?"

"Colin was found dead this morning," Jordan said. "Do you have any idea if he had any plans last night, if he was meeting anyone?"

The roommate, Jeffrey Bishop, shook his head. "Nope, he didn't talk to me about these things. We've been sharing a room for the past two years—he doesn't say much at all, is always studying...was," he corrected himself solemnly. "I don't think he went to any party in his time here."

Jordan shared another look with Derek, suppressing the urge to shake her head. Apparently, Bishop thought of this as a big loss.

"Wow," he said, "that's really bad. Was he robbed?"

"Can you tell us when you last saw him?"

"He was in class yesterday afternoon. That's the last time."

"Did you see him talk to anyone?"

"No, but that's not unusual. He goes straight to the library."

"Thank you. We'll check that."

Jordan could tell that Bishop was still mulling this over, seeming more surprised than shocked that his roommate had been killed. She waited.

"Um...I don't know if that's important to you."

"Just tell me. We'll sort it out later."

Bishop took a deep breath. "I mean I wasn't surprised that he didn't have lots of friends here, he was just that type...but he got some text messages at night the past few weeks, and one time, a guy came and asked for him...Colin wasn't here."

"Okay. Can you describe the guy?"

His reaction was the shrug she got from too many witnesses. "Dark hair, tall, good looking...not who you'd think Colin would hang out with."

Because stereotypes were well and alive in this school, too, Jordan thought, barely suppressing a sigh. "If you could come to the station for a facial composite later, it would be very helpful."

"With a sketch artist?" he asked, intrigued.

"It's all computerized now, but yes, it's the same principle."

"Sure, when do you want me there?"

They settled on five-thirty and afterwards, made a detour to the library on the way out where the librarian confirmed that Colin had come by after his class, but left after getting a call, around six.

"You know this for sure?" Jordan asked, surprised.

"Oh yes," the woman said. "He was very dedicated. I saw him here almost every day, and he was always immersed in his studies, rarely speaking to anyone. This was the first time I had to remind him to turn his phone off."

They had yet to find his cell phone.

"He's very eager to help. You think he knows more that he's telling us?" Derek asked with regard to the roommate.

"Not sure, but I would like to find out who that tall dark-haired stranger is. The sooner we get that composite, the better."

"A lover?"

"Let's not get ahead of ourselves. I'd like to stop at Darla's before we go back. She knows the neighborhood pretty well."

⁓

Darla had some time before her work shift started, and she agreed to meet them. Taking in the small, but cozy apartment, Jordan felt assured that Darla had made herself at home in a new, better reality.

"You'd like to hold him for a moment?" Not indulging her indecisiveness for long, Darla handed her baby boy to Jordan before she straightened the blankets in his bed. Jordan tried to focus on what she'd come here for in the first place. Holding the baby in her arms was deceptively calming, and the workday was nowhere near over.

"Thanks."

Finally, Darla straightened, and her tone and expression seemed a lot more like the woman Jordan had come to know earlier in their relationship. "What do you want to know?"

She didn't flinch when Jordan showed her the picture. Jordan hadn't expected her to. Darla had seen bad, and worse.

"Wrong neighborhood, huh? Bad coincidence, or was he looking for something?"

"Any idea what he could have hoped to find? Neighbor talked about a group of guys hanging around, with baseball caps and jerseys, one of them with the number six."

It was a long shot—Darla lived a different life now, and she might not appreciate the reminder.

"Number six," she said. "That's blatant. I'm not sure, but I might be able to help you find him."

"Wait, just like that? #6, it's a thing?"

"Oh yes, people know him around. I'm surprised you didn't hear of him. Guy's so full of himself, it's a miracle he's not in jail yet."

"You got a real name?"

"Chucky somebody, but I'll get you in touch with someone who can probably give you a last name too."

"Really? I don't want you to do anything dangerous, you hear me? Let us take care of this."

Darla's wry smile reminded her of what they both knew—their previous arrangement had without a doubt been dangerous, and both of them had accepted the premise. That had been a different time though. They both had been different people.

"I'm not going to do anything stupid, especially now. I'll make a few calls, and if I find out anything, I'll get right back to you. I promise."

When Jordan obviously didn't convey enough confidence, Darla added, "Take a look around. I'm a mom. I have a job and a roof over our heads. There's no way I'll put any of that at risk. I can ask a few people who might know what #6 is doing now. He used to do a bit of everything, drugs, gambling, girls. Not as big as Ryder..." She shuddered at the memory. "But enough to make a splash. Last thing I heard he was laying low, but with Ryder and his gang in prison now, I assume he wants to get his share back. To your original question, it's likely that your college boy was looking for ways to get high or get laid, and he ran into some bad luck."

"Thank you. That's more than I hoped for, actually."

"You're welcome. You know, if you want to do me a favor, donuts are always a good idea."

"I'll remember that. Excuse me," Jordan said when her cell phone rang, and she turned away while Derek made some small talk with Darla.

"I'm sorry for calling you in the middle of the day."

"That's fine, Ariel, are you okay?"

"No." The girl's voice sounded tearful. "You said I could always talk to you or Ellie. Could you come see me? Soon?"

"Sure, I can come by later this evening. Is it about the trial? I know you're scared, but they can't do anything to you. There will be lots of police." Jordan knew this couldn't be much of a consolation for Ariel when she had to face the father who didn't want her—which was, all things considered, still a blessing—and potentially the man who had killed her mother. A.D.A. Esposito would do her best to keep them apart, but the men on trial had expensive lawyers on their side.

"I know. I don't really want to do this, but I know I have to."

"You won't be the only one." Some of the women in the cult had agreed to testify as well, but most of them were either too intimidated or had been conditioned from an early age to support the men no matter what. Jordan didn't blame them, but that didn't mean she wasn't angry or frustrated at the status quo which put lots of pressure on a traumatized teen. "I promise, I'll come by later tonight, and then we'll talk some more. Is that okay with you?"

"Yeah. I guess. Thank you."

"No problem. I'll check in with Ellie, and maybe she'll have time too."

"I read about this online," Darla said after Jordan had ended the call. "What a bunch of assholes. It's good you shut them down."

Jordan wasn't going to argue with any of it.

"Call me when you have something. I owe you."

Darla chuckled. "Just like old times, huh?"

It was Jordan's turn to barely suppress a shudder. She preferred to think of the future these days.

Chapter Four

E llie had spent most of the day with a sense of disbelief. She had made a plan. She had always been a planner but became even more meticulous and disciplined about her goals after her parents' death. Because life was short, and every moment counted. She hadn't allowed the man who attacked her on the street one night, to stop her, other than the few days she'd had to spend in the hospital. Even when he came back to abduct her, she had refused to give him power over her life in the aftermath.

She had wanted Jordan. To become a detective. To land a job with Homicide—and after everything she'd invested, it wasn't fair that this should be the time all her careful planning came to a jarring halt. Ellie knew for certain that she hadn't made a mistake. It was her calling. It was where she belonged. But the precinct had chosen someone else over her, and at her current workplace, Waters showed no signs of retiring anytime soon.

Ellie never allowed herself to remain in a state of dissatisfaction for long, because there was always something to do, something to work toward...Still, she found herself sitting in the bistro for a late lunch, picking at her salad she didn't want to order in the first place. Then again, since she was still wearing the uniform, a big piece of pastry and a red wine like she craved wouldn't have been the best choice in public. She knew she'd get over it because she always had.

All her recent achievements, though, professional and personal, couldn't do away with the facts. The attack and subsequent abduction had changed her. Ellie still had nightmares at times, and she knew they might never go away completely. She and Jordan were going to buy a house together, but that didn't promise them permanence. And whichever great things she was going to do with her life, her parents were still dead.

Ellie felt the tears burning behind her eyes. She tossed a bill on the table and left her uneaten meal, heading back to her car where she wiped her face angrily. This wasn't her. She didn't give up, didn't dwell. There would be another opportunity. There had to be.

She found the text message from Jordan a few minutes later. They would meet at the station after their respective work shifts and then go see Ariel.

Perhaps it wasn't such a bad idea to remind herself that someone had it worse—being as young as she was, Ariel had a lot less control over her life. Ellie wished she could help her more than the occasional phone call or visit. She wasn't sure how.

In any case, she had decided, she would do her job best she could, go the extra mile even if that involved some unusual tasks.

"I'm so sorry to bother you," the young mother who had called them, said while her daughter was sobbing. "She's been up there for over an hour, and we didn't know what to do." "She" was the kitten the family had gotten for the girl's birthday and had recently explored the tree across the street, getting too high up to find a way back on her own.

"That's all right," Casey assured her. "I'm going to call the fire department. They take care of these things...Ellie?"

"Come on. We don't need to call them for that."

Ellie hadn't climbed a tree in some time, but she didn't see any reason for wasting time and resources on this rather easy task. Ignoring Casey's disbelief, she reached for the cat that didn't show much appreciation for her rescue efforts.

"Don't do this," Ellie spoke to her. "I know it's tempting to cling to a bad situation, but you'd rather want to be with the people down there. Right?"

She didn't need to see it to know Casey was rolling her eyes. "Come on, kitty. I don't have all day, and—ouch. No, definitely don't do that."

Finally, the cat was giving up her resistance. Ellie could carefully climb back down and hand it to the girl.

"Thank you so much!" She gave both Ellie and her cat an enthusiastic hug.

"You're welcome. What is your name?"

"Sandy."

"All right, Sandy. You promise me to take good care of that kitten?"

The girl nodded.

"Can you tell me what that was?" Casey asked when they were back in the car.

"Saving another kitten? That's what I do now, apparently."

"Come on, Harding, what's the matter with you?"

"What do you mean? It's part of the job. I'd feel silly waiting for the fire department to show up."

Another call came over dispatch, a home invasion in progress. Ellie answered it, and they were on their way.

The balcony of the apartment door stood open, and they could hear drawers and cabinet doors being opened. A man had climbed over the ground floor railing and entered the apartment, according to the witness. The neighbor didn't know whether or not the tenant was inside.

"Thank you, Ma'am. Please stay inside now. Okay," Ellie said after the door closed. "Let's find out what's going on here."

"I'll call for—damn it, Ellie," Casey whispered before she followed her onto the small balcony and into the living room. A staircase led to an upper level. Carefully, they made it from the living room towards the source of the noise.

The bedroom door was ajar, and the intruder was inside, turning over the mattress.

"Police! Put your hands up!" Ellie yelled at him. He stood frozen, not reacting to her command either. Her gaze fell onto the bundles of money under the mattress. This home obviously belonged to someone who didn't trust banks, and chances were, the robber had known about it.

"I said hands up!"

He finally complied long enough for her to cuff him, and Ellie breathed a sigh of relief—only to jump at the sound from another room a moment later. Judging from Casey's stormy look, she probably wished Ellie would have given her the time to call for backup.

"Is anyone up here? Hello?"

Assured that Casey had her eyes on the robber, Ellie peeked outside the door, holstering her weapon again when she saw a man in boxer shorts coming from a bathroom at the end of the hall.

"It's all right. We got the intruder, Mr....?"

"Lansing. Wow." He raked a hand through his hair. "I better put on some pants. I came out of the shower when I heard the sounds, and I thought it was safer to stay in here and call you. Thank you."

"You did the right thing. One of your neighbors notified us as well. We'll just wait for my colleagues now. You can go and get dressed in the meantime."

"Thanks so much."

Five minutes later, backup had arrived, and Casey took Ellie aside.

"What is it with you today?"

"What do you mean? The guy might have gotten away if we waited."

"We were also lucky that there was just one guy."

Ellie shrugged. "The neighbor told dispatch she saw one man breaking in. What do you want me to say?"

"Follow protocol the next time?"

Today of all days, Ellie wasn't in the mood to argue. "Sure thing," she said.

"Good."

❧

After Bishop had completed the composite, Jordan sent the graphic to Darla just in case.

Sorry, that's not #6, a text message reached her minutes later. *He doesn't look familiar.*

No problem. Thanks.

In passing, she heard Officer Chris Atwood laughing. "I hear Bristol is giving Harding a piece of his mind. Can't seem to follow orders, that one. It's a miracle she made it as far as she has—well, not really." Jordan turned to glare at him, but he was already walking away. So, Ellie's day hadn't gotten better, though she had confirmed earlier that she'd accompany Jordan to the home Ariel was living in.

Jordan decided to find her and try to lift her mood some before they went to see the girl.

She ran into Ellie on the way to the area where the interrogation rooms were located. Perfect.

"Hey, I'm almost done, but there's something I wanted to show you."

Ellie sighed. "Please tell me it's something good. It's already been a terrible day."

"I'm sorry I had to hang up on you earlier—and that you didn't get the job," Jordan said when Ellie walked back with her. "They have no idea what they're missing."

"Well, not according to Casey and Sergeant Bristol. I mean, come on, one guy looking for money and jewelry, and we could catch him right in the act. That kitten on the tree put up more resistance."

"Do I want to know?" Jordan asked, not sure whether it was appropriate to laugh. Taking in the scratches on Ellie's hand, she winced. The kitten on the tree had not been a metaphor. "Wow. You climbed a tree?"

"Why not?"

Jordan didn't think she needed to continue down that road. She opened the door to the observation area.

"What is this?" Ellie asked when she saw that the interrogation room was empty.

She didn't question Jordan's motives any longer when Jordan pushed her lightly against the wall and kissed her. She relaxed in Jordan's embrace, and this time, her sigh didn't come from frustration.

"Better?" Jordan whispered.

Ellie leaned against the wall, smiling. "Much better. It's a miracle."

"I'm glad. I know it's been a rough day. We've had some of those. There will be another opening."

"Yeah, sure. Did you hear from Andrea?"

"Oh, that's right, yes. She has another house for us, and she promised that we'll be able to afford it."

Ellie laughed. "Do we have to build it ourselves?"

"Come on, it won't be that bad. A few renos, she said, but it's in the location we want."

"Okay. That sounds good. Thank you." Ellie leaned forward to kiss her on the lips. This time, the contact was brief. Their day wasn't over yet. "What's going on with Ariel?"

"I don't know yet, but I think she's nervous about the trial. I thought we might be able to ease her mind a bit."

"Yes, let's do that. I'll change, and then we can go. We could take her out to dinner if the folks from the home allow it. I'm starving."

"Me too. Hurry up."

❧

Like so many times in the past few months...like every day, Jonathan Darby thought of his last subject, the one who not only escaped, but had rescued another woman, found one more alive. He had every reason to hate Jordan Carpenter, for interfering with his mission, but still, he was strangely fascinated by her.

Many exciting things were happening at once, and his only regret was that he might not be around long enough to see them come to fruition.

Ironic, wasn't it.

He had brought punishment to many, often by death...now death was catching up to him.

Not yet, though.

He stroked a fingertip over the grainy black and white picture.

He thought of the young girl Jordan had rescued from the cult, already tainted by the sins of her mother. There was something about the story that intrigued him. In their midst, there had been one like him. His story had come to an end, not so Jonathan Darby's.

He would die, but he'd still win.

"You're still my favorite," he said, smiling to himself.

Chapter Five

"We already had dinner," Marla Sherman who ran the group home, said. "I'm sorry. It would be better if you called ahead, and besides, it's important for Ariel to socialize with the other kids here."

"I understand. We'd still like to see her," Jordan insisted. There was nothing sinister about this place, just people who tried to do their job best they could. Still, she felt uncomfortable every time she set foot in here, and Ellie's concerned gaze told her that she knew.

She'd only spent a brief time in a home like this before her placement with Pauline and Jack Carpenter proved to be the perfect solution for everyone involved. Jordan remembered well how all she'd wanted was for the noise to stop, to be left in peace. That need for peace, quiet and space, had persisted into her adult years.

"Of course. Is there anything we need to know? About the trial? The A.D.A. was here too."

"Ariel is well prepared for the trial," Ellie said. "We'd just like to check on her."

"All right. She is in her room. Come with me."

They walked up one flight of stairs and along a hallway, and then Ms. Sherman knocked on Ariel's door.

"Ariel? You have visitors." She turned to Jordan and Ellie, saying, "Before you go, could you please stop by my office?"

"Sure. Hi Ariel," Jordan said after they'd closed the door. "How are you doing?"

"You're here," Ariel said as if she couldn't believe they'd actually answered her plea. "I'm...fine." Her smile wasn't quite convincing. After everything she'd been through, this wasn't a surprise, but at least she was safe here.

Was she?

"That's good. Did anyone of your family try to contact you?"

Ariel shook her head. "Most of them think I'm a traitor, and the rest are too busy with themselves to care. I...I'm sorry I bothered you. I shouldn't have."

Ellie exchanged a look with Jordan before she said, "We really meant it. When we said we wanted to keep in touch. It's not just about work, or your testimony. We want to make sure you're okay."

"Why?" Ariel asked, her eyes welling up. "Why would you care when even my family doesn't?"

Jordan had never asked that question out loud, but she sure had mulled it over a lot after she moved in with Jack and Pauline, even years after those first days. Even now, she wasn't sure she had a good answer. Ellie beat her to it.

"Because you're an amazing person who has been through something terrible. Nobody should have to experience that, but at least, when we do, someone should care, make sure you have what you need to be okay."

"Are you?" Ariel asked. "Did it stop hurting so bad eventually?"

"Yes," Ellie said without reservation. "And it doesn't mean you forget about your mom and all she did for you, on the contrary. I didn't know her, but the agent I worked with did.

40

She tried to get both of you out. The best way to honor her is to carry on and be with people who care."

"You mean like here?"

There was something about her tone Jordan didn't like. "The people here, they treat you okay?"

Ariel shrugged. "I guess so."

"Did anyone say or do something inappropriate?"

"No, I just think they have no idea what it was like with the Prophets. They try. I guess that counts."

Jordan couldn't shake the feeling that there had been another reason for Ariel to call, and that she wouldn't share it tonight. Maybe Ms. Sherman could shed more light on the situation.

"Whatever happens, you know you can always call, right? Ms. Sherman said we could have lunch or dinner sometime if you like."

"Really? That would be awesome." Ariel's enthusiasm vanished quickly. "I guess you have to go now. I'll see you at the trial then?"

"I'm sure we'll find some time before that. Have a good night."

"You too. Thanks for coming." Jordan was surprised to find herself enveloped in a tight hug the next moment.

❦

Ellie had enjoyed the way Jordan tried to lighten up her mood earlier. Outside of those moments, the hits just kept on coming.

"Ariel is quiet and polite whenever you speak to her, but she has trouble with structure and rules."

Jordan's gaze conveyed her disbelief. Ellie wasn't sure what to make of this either.

"That's...a surprise. She's lived with extreme structure and rules all her life."

"The emphasis being on extreme. Children differ in how they deal with a situation like this, but from what we know, being a girl, she faced threats constantly. She saw how the grown women were treated by the brothers, and she witnessed all of that being trapped in a rigorous day-to-day routine. Obviously, we don't operate that way here, but we do need some rules. Ariel is late for meals, for sessions, just about everything. You saw her room all cleaned up? She usually doesn't keep it that way, and she always finds an excuse."

"Her mother was murdered." Jordan's tone was quiet, but Ellie could detect the underlying emotions, anger being one of them.

"I'm not telling you this out of a lack of empathy. Many of the children here have faced trauma, and we have staff to deal with that. I want you to know the facts. It's not unusual for her to act out like that."

"Are you any closer to placing her in a family?"

Ms. Sherman looked doubtful. "It's a complicated situation. Her father has stated clearly that he has no interest in raising her, but there might be other family members coming forward. We can't really say until after the trial. Not every single man and woman will be convicted or found unfit to parent."

"So, meanwhile, what are you going to do?"

"We try to be as strict as we possibly can, try to teach her the difference between the only life she knows, and one where being part of a group serves her too. She needs real stability. So—I was hoping you could continue to visit after the trial."

"That's the plan," Ellie said. "We really want to make sure she's okay."

"All right then. Thanks for your time. I think her testimony will lift a huge weight off her shoulders."

Ellie and Jordan walked out of the building in silence, each lost in her own thoughts.

Was this the end of the road, all they could do for the girl, check in every once in a while, until one family member remembered her? It didn't seem enough.

❧

Darla came through and found them a friend of hers who had seen #6 and was willing to talk to the police. Meanwhile, the autopsy on Colin Buck gave them an approximate time of death. He'd been shot in the chest twice at close range, no signs of a struggle. His last meal had been at a fast-food joint, and no drugs or alcohol had been found in his system.

"What if he was dealing?" A.D.A. Valerie Esposito asked when Jordan updated her and the lieutenant in his office.

"If that was the case, he had to have been extremely careful. There were no signs whatsoever in his dorm room, or from his finances. I think we can learn more from Chucky Mulveney a.k.a. #6."

"Sound like he's quite the character. I agree," Valerie said. "Let's get you that warrant and see what he has to say. Come with me?"

"Sure."

When they were alone in her office, Valerie surprisingly changed the subject.

"So, what's up with the Deane girl?"

"What do you mean? You don't have to worry. No one's going to interfere with the case. We want these guys behind bars as much as you do."

"I don't doubt that. I just think it's curious. You don't still check in with Judy Lawrence?"

The stab of guilt didn't make any sense. "No, because the case is closed, and she has her own life. She's not a minor. It doesn't mean I don't care."

"You care a lot about Ariel," Valerie said quietly. "Because you were in her place?"

"My mother is alive, thank you very much. My birthmother is too. No, I wasn't in her place."

"You know what I mean. I want you to be careful. You're becoming too attached."

"How about you get me that warrant now?"

Valerie shook her head.

"You're still doing that thing. Yes, I'll get you the warrant."

"What thing?" Jordan asked, irritated. Valerie had the phone already in hand and put it back down.

"Don't act like you don't know. That thing where you bail in the middle of a conversation because it hits too close to home. Well, at least it's not my problem. As long as little Ariel delivers her statement as planned, we're good. Let me make that call now, then you can go talk to Pierson's friend and hopefully bring in the guy in the jersey before lunch."

Jordan waited, not willing to waste any time on a response, though she was mildly offended by Valerie's interpretation. She wasn't that bad at communicating, was she? She'd take Ellie's word over that of a woman she'd once had a brief and inconsequential affair with.

⟡

Kim Geller worked in a hair salon downtown. She stepped outside to talk to Jordan and Derek and have a cigarette at the same time. It might not be Geller's intention, but the wind blew cigarette smoke in Jordan's face constantly. Suppressing a cough, she said, "Darla told us you know where #6 is?"

"He certainly thinks of himself as #1," the woman said with disdain. "I've been working here for two years now, and he thinks now that Ryder is out, he can come back and harass me.

There are poker games at Rigley's every Friday. He never misses one of them."

"Did he threaten you?" Jordan wanted to know.

"He's got a big mouth," Kim didn't quite answer her question. "I'll be fine."

"Okay, but I'd like you to stay under the radar for the time being. Here's my card. If he or one of his friends come around, you call me."

She shrugged but took the card. "Yeah, whatever."

"Thanks, Kim. I appreciate it."

Derek's cell phone rang, and he stepped aside to answer the call. He ended it a couple of minutes later, looking somber when he joined her in the car.

Jordan waited. When he remained quiet after a long, awkward moment, she said, "You're going to share or not?" Realization dawned, and she shook her head. "Kate? I'm sorry, that's none of my business."

"No, it's about Buck," he said. "That was the lab, something they found on his laptop. It's odd. Apparently, there was no official record of this, but he seems to have done an internship with a lawyer. At least that's how I'd interpret the money he was paid, not in his bank account, but with an online provider."

"You're speaking in riddles."

"Colin Buck appears to have had some sort of gig with Mr. Donovan."

Jordan didn't need any more explanations. "Damn it." Somehow, that wasn't strong enough an expletive, so she tried another one. "Fuck." Getting closer.

"I'm sorry. I can go see him if you—"

"I don't mind seeing Donovan," she interrupted him. "In fact, let's get this over with right now."

"It might not be a coincidence that he brought you the letter."

"Come on. The guy's in prison. He's dying. He's not the all-powerful mastermind you make him out to be. There's nothing he could do from prison."

"I didn't say Darby did anything, but he could have an admirer. Someone who's connected to Buck, Donovan and Mulveney."

"And to think that going to a poker game would be the low point of my week." Jordan leaned back in her seat with a sigh. "Okay. Donovan first, afterwards we check out Rigley's."

Donovan, who had represented Jonathan Darby after his arrest, was in his office when they arrived, and agreed to see them right away.

"Detective Carpenter, I'm surprised to see you here. Did you change your mind on—"

"Colin Buck," she said. "I assume you heard about his death."

Donovan's eyes widened. "The college student? He hasn't come in for a while, didn't leave a message, so I assumed he had lost interest. That's awful."

"It sure is. Mr. Donovan, what exactly was the nature of Mr. Buck's employment with you? You paid him via *moneymonkey*?" Derek couldn't hide the frown at the provider's name. "You use it for all of your financial transactions?"

Jordan had always disliked Donovan, the way he seemed to be able to put aside easily everything Darby had done. He had been too interested in details of each woman's story, including hers. However, she noticed he gave Derek the same condescending smile.

"Of course not, Detective. Colin asked me to, and I saw no reason to reject his wish."

Just like when Darby asked you to deliver the letter? Always willing to help.

"Colin needed a job, and I needed some help, someone who could make copies, carry files, take notes. He wanted to be a lawyer."

The next question was obvious. Jordan was grateful that Derek asked it anyway.

"Was he in any way involved with Jonathan Darby's case?"

"Mr. Darby's case, and other cases. He would accompany me at times, especially when I was asked to settle Mr. Darby's affairs."

"So they met?" Derek exchanged a quick look with Jordan, and she agreed that this was curious.

"You could barely call it that. In any case, Colin was there to observe and take notes. You're not alleging that Mr. Darby is responsible for Colin's murder? With all due respect, Detective Carpenter, but that's a reach. The man is sick. He has a few months, maybe."

"Excuse me if I can't be too sad about it," Jordan said coolly. "No, we don't think Darby murdered him, but he might know who did. You brought me the letter. It had some ominous message."

"Did it refer to your case specifically? Or Colin Buck?"

"No. That doesn't mean—"

"I'm a little busy. I can assure you, Colin always did what was asked of him, copies, coffee, filing, a little bit of everything. He informed himself about all my clients, but he didn't show a specific interest in Mr. Darby, not more than the general public, anyway. If that's all, Detectives, I need to get back to work. Unless you're accusing me of something, I'll have to ask you to leave."

"We'll be in touch," Jordan said, which was mostly for the heck of it. She didn't believe that Donovan would tell them anything else. Darby...They couldn't trust any word that was coming out of his mouth.

A few months.

"Let's drive by Rigley's and then head back, see if they have anything else on the laptop."

"You know we have to check…"

"Yes." Jordan knew that the only way to get to Darby was with a strategy. He obviously wanted to trick her into seeing him, but there was no way she was getting into a room with him if there wasn't a real quid pro quo—something good, something that would help her solve this case. "We'll figure something out."

Chapter Six

I f she asked the lieutenant for an appointment, a few minutes of his time, Ellie thought she might be able to make her case. Even if there wasn't an opening right now, she didn't want to miss her chance once the moment came. She wanted her potential future boss to know that she was determined, and that she had an interest in staying with this precinct. Lastly, she was no stranger to him, and it was an advantage to hire from within. All of this made perfect sense in her head, but she was still feeling on edge. The unresolved situation with Ariel weighed on her as well.

Jordan should have a slower day, as they were setting up the sting to catch Chucky Mulveney at the poker game on Friday. She was confident about the outcome, given that Darla's information had always been good.

Ellie felt an urgency she couldn't quite explain, a feeling that had grown infinitely stronger since the interview hadn't gone as she'd hoped. Casey had noticed it too.

It had been an unusually busy morning, but maybe it was busier than most because Ellie had all but jumped on every call.

"I think it's lunchtime," Casey reminded her gently.

"But..." Ellie wished she hadn't mentioned lunch. Her stomach growled.

"See, we're not even that close," Casey pointed out when another unit answered the call.

"What if they need someone else—?"

Ellie's question was answered by yet another unit signaling they were on their way.

"Unless someone says 'all available units,' and that didn't happen, I'm stepping out of this car right now. We haven't stopped for a minute. I need to pee, and you need to chill."

If there was something funny to this, Ellie didn't quite see the humor, but she followed Casey out of the car and across the street into the diner. Casey went to the restroom while Ellie sat at the counter, picked up a menu and laid it down immediately.

She didn't understand why she was feeling so restless, so uncomfortable with the delay of her plans. She was going to move in with Jordan, and the shared mortgage wouldn't be much more than what she was paying for rent now. She had passed the exam with flying colors just like she'd known she would, like everyone had expected. She might be able to work in another department, just not Homicide at this time, or she could wait it out, right?

Casey frowned when she returned and saw that Ellie had nothing but a coffee in front of her. "What is up with you?" she asked.

"Nothing. I don't like wasting time, that's all."

"You can't be serious. What do you mean by wasting time anyway? Having lunch?"

"No, of course not."

"Then what is it?"

"I don't know. It doesn't matter. Let's eat something so we can get out of here."

Casey's look spoke volumes, but she stopped trying to press Ellie for an answer.

"Yeah. Let's eat."

Jordan hadn't told Ellie what the plan was. She didn't want her to worry when they both had a lot on their mind regardless of whatever game Darby was playing. After all, it was Derek who was going to interview him, not her, and chances were she wouldn't have to go anywhere near him. This was a loose end they had to tie up, but she didn't expect anything substantial to come out of it. Check the box. Move on.

She was in another room, following the interview from a safe distance on a monitor. Nevertheless, Jordan flinched when on the screen, the door was opened, and Darby shuffled into the room. He looked a decade older than when she'd last seen him.

His face fell when he saw Derek.

"Mr. Darby. I have a few questions regarding a student who accompanied your attorney a few times, Colin Buck."

"I imagine. I had hoped to see Jordan?"

He would try, any way, to get a rise out of Derek, knowing the anger simmering just underneath Derek's cool façade.

"We can't always get what we hope for, can we? Did you ever talk to Mr. Buck?"

"A couple of times," Darby said, smiling cordially. "Yes, I remember him, a nice young man. He had many questions." He turned his gaze to the camera in the corner of the ceiling. "Is she here?"

"What kind of questions?"

"I'm sure she is. Jordan, I want you to know I've been thinking about you."

No surprise so far.

"I was told you were going to answer questions. This is a waste of time." Derek got to his feet, letting the chair scrape across the floor.

"You're leaving already? You don't want to know what Colin asked me?"

"I know that you're lying. Donovan told us Buck took notes, that he barely talked to you."

"Detective Henderson! Wait! I don't know why he would say that. He even agreed to give Colin and me some privacy, so we could discuss...matters. You talked to Donovan? He gave Jordan the letter? Look, I'm going to tell you. I get mail from admirers. Mostly women, but some men too—I guess they have a bit of a crush. Colin was one of them, and he took the job so he could meet me in person."

Derek gave an incredulous laugh.

"Yeah, right. I have other things to do than to listen to this shit."

Jordan wasn't so sure anymore.

"Ah, come on, it wasn't anything sexual. He was interested in my story."

"Why would I believe you, when we found nothing in his room, or on his computer to back up that fantasy of yours?"

Jordan could have given the answer even before Darby spoke.

"He was a law student. His interests were a bit risqué, so he couldn't exactly brag about them on social media. That is dark net stuff—you know, the place where I interacted with Dr. Roberts."

Derek looked slightly sick at the reminder of the way Bethany had laid out her trap, and the way it had backfired. Jordan couldn't blame him.

"If you dig deeper, you'll find something. When you do, I might have something else for you."

"Which is what?"

"No, not that fast. You're going to find proof of Colin's...admiration for me, and then you'll come back. I'll give you more if I can talk to Jordan."

"Oh, for Pete's sake." In the other room, Jordan groaned. This was disappointingly predictable. He couldn't do better than that?

"That's not going to happen."

"No? Jordan, if you can hear this, what if it's bigger than just one screwed up college kid? Wouldn't you like to know?"

Here we go.

"There are many lost souls out there," he said, turning his gaze back on Derek. "I have a front row seat, unfortunately, not for much longer. I am willing to help you, though, not because I want to make amends, but to avoid someone else crapping all over my legacy while I'm still here." Gone was the conversational tone, the smile. Jordan remembered that Jonathan Darby too, and it worried her. Could it be that he knew something? It didn't make sense, or maybe she didn't want it to make sense. Donovan had built his career on impossible high-profile cases. He wouldn't want to trash it because of one serial killer? There was nothing Darby could have promised him.

"I give you one more thing. Colin had some unusual friends. Come back soon, please. I'll be waiting."

Derek glared at the laughing man, before he turned to leave. A few second later, he joined Jordan.

"What a bunch of crap," he said, sounding disgusted. Jordan watched as Darby was led back to his cell. He smiled, raising his shackled hands as if to wave at her.

"I'm not so sure," she said before turning off the monitor.

"Oh no, don't tell me you fell for that."

"Remember what Bishop told us? The guy who was asking for Colin?"

"Yeah. I wouldn't be surprised if he's connected to Chucky #6 somehow, but this has nothing to do with Darby. You were right about the letter. All he wants is to rattle you."

"I'm not sure we can take that chance, but we'll see what the lab can tell us and go from there."

That was something they could agree on.

⁓

After chasing a man, who had robbed a jewelry store, down several blocks, even Ellie had to admit she was ready to call it a day. Sorting out her notes at her desk after they'd brought the robber down to booking, she decided to wait for Jordan and go to the *Night Shift* from here. Casey regarded her thoughtfully before she said, "I'll see you later?"

"You certainly will. I'll just finish up here."

Spontaneously, she picked up the phone and called Ariel's home.

Sherman informed her that the girls were having dinner at the moment, and nothing had changed as to Ariel's conduct. Ellie hung up with a sigh. She was certain that the other side would want to hear Ms. Sherman's and other experts' testimony on Ariel's credibility, and she hoped Ariel's issues in dealing with the unexpected freedom wouldn't be a problem.

"Hey. You're still here."

"Yeah, just waiting for Jordan," she answered her friend Libby. "You're going to the *Night Shift*?"

"In a bit, yes. Did you hear anything from Kate?"

"Nothing since the last text. I guess she needed that time-out," Ellie said, and Libby nodded.

She was glad Kate was doing something for herself. It was long overdue. What did she need? Ellie asked herself. Was she acting selfish?

"What about you? I heard you've been busy. Not that I doubt it, we've barely seen you. You and Jordan are still looking for a house?"

"Oh yes." Ellie felt her features relax into a smile. "We're going to see something next week."

"Cool. I look forward to the housewarming party."

"Party? What's the occasion?"

Jordan had only overheard the last part of Libby's sentence.

"I'll leave that up to you, Ellie. See you later."

Ellie took one last look at her notes and got up. "Let's go. It's been one of those days."

"No kidding," Jordan said, and it occurred to Ellie that she looked tired. "So, what was that about a party? Not today, please."

"No, not today. But hopefully soon."

⁓

Jordan was still mulling over the preliminary results from the lab when they sat at the table with a group of friends. Colin Buck's internet footprint was unassuming. A private Facebook and Twitter account, nothing remarkable there.

Darby might have lied. He might have told the truth, and Buck had sought out employment with Donovan specifically. Donovan's name had been in the press in connection with Darby's a lot. If he had indeed used other channels to satisfy his interest in Darby and his crimes, it would take a lot longer to find. She would have to do some research on the fans of serial killers, their online hangouts, see if there was one group that had welcomed Colin in their midst.

This should be fun.

"Hey, Carpenter, you have a moment?"

Casey Lyons startled her out of her musings. Ellie was standing at the bar with Libby Marshall, immersed in conversation.

"Sure."

Casey cast a look at Ellie before she said, "I was hoping you could tell me what's the matter with her?"

"Ellie? Why?" Jordan asked, confused. "If this is about the job, you should talk to her first."

"Yes and no. She's been a little off lately. She was really thrilled after she took the exam."

"Yeah, well, there isn't an opening right now. I think it's justified that she's a little disappointed."

"I understand that. In the past few days, she's been a bit...intense."

Intense was a way to describe Ellie on any day. Jordan still didn't get what the problem was.

"Look, I appreciate your concern, but you don't have to worry. We're fine, Ellie's fine, but there's a lot going on right now, with the cult case coming to court and all. Ellie's doing her job, and she's good at it. Right?"

"Yeah." Casey took a sip of her beer. "Forget I said anything. I'd be disappointed too. She's worked hard for this."

"No harm done."

"Friday's still poker night?" Casey asked.

"Yep. Let's hope we get lucky."

"You can get lucky tonight," Ellie who had returned, said. "Oops. Casey."

"Yeah, me." Casey shook her head with a smile. "I realize I'm not needed here. Thanks for the advice, Jordan. Good night."

"What was that about?"

"Nothing in particular. She had some questions about the sting."

Ellie slipped back into the booth, leaning against her. "We should have picked the *D&T* tonight. Sometimes, it's a good idea to take a break from the shop talk."

"Speaking of which, you promised me something..."

"I did…and I plan to deliver." Ellie leaned in to kiss her. So easy, those little sins of omission—but Jordan was certain she'd done the right thing. The last thing she needed was to add any more stress for either of them.

Chapter Seven

D onovan didn't seem the least bit concerned when they confronted him with Darby's statement, slightly contradicting his own.

"Mr. Donovan," Derek said, "Mr. Darby told us that there were regular conversations between him and Colin during those visits. Now, they might be privileged, but it's still curious."

"What's curious about that? He's my client, but it's no secret that the man is a liar and a psychopath. Messing with people is his favorite pastime."

"Oh, that's a cute way to say it." Jordan couldn't help it.

"Like it or not, but it's true."

"All right then. We'll be in touch."

"If you must," Donovan said. "I'm not sure what you're thinking, but I can't imagine Colin conversing with Mr. Darby. That boy was always so nervous, he would have peed his pants."

"Thanks for your time, anyway."

In the following days, techs tried to trace Colin's steps in darker areas of the world wide web, with little to no success. If he had any odd affinity to serial killers, he had covered his tracks well. The only hint was that he'd done some research on Darby, which was nothing surprising given his assignment. But why be so secretive about it?

Jordan had spent the better part of the past days looking at groups that had an interest in serial killers, Darby specifically. There was one claiming that he never even existed, and the whole case was one big government conspiracy. She sighed in frustration, shaking her head at the screen.

"It's too early for this shit—again," she said to herself. Then again, there was never a good time to search for the needle in a dirty, stinking haystack.

Derek who had come in cast a look over her shoulder. "Let me guess. Alien zombie Elvis did it?"

"Something like that. It's no big deal that one person puts up a site like this. The number of followers...That's terrifying."

"No kidding."

There was another group called The Real & True Conversation that saw a connection between moral decay in society, and Darby's crimes.

"Right. How is killing people morally superior?" Since Derek already agreed with her, this was a rather rhetorical question, but Jordan needed a moment to vent. "I'll be so happy when we don't have to deal with this crap any longer. A few months, and this is going to be over. *He* is going to be over." She flinched when a photo of herself came up, in a folder with Judy Lawrence, Lori Gleason, and women who were dead. The members of the group claimed, while not condoning murder and torture, to carry on a philosophical discussion on how taboos kept society working. The mere idea that someone thought Darby had a point, even if they objected to the way he'd been making it, turned her stomach.

"I believe you that those people are sick...but do we have anything on Colin Buck?"

Jordan shrugged. "Not yet. At this point, it's still fishing."

"Maybe it's time to let go. Darby sold us a load of bull. As usual."

"I don't know. He knows I'm not going to set foot in there if he doesn't give us something."

"So? Maybe making you think that he has something, that you might have to do this, is enough for him? How well did you sleep last night?"

She yawned, not elaborating that she wasn't tired because of nightmares. "I guess there's your answer. Get me some coffee, please? I'd really appreciate it."

Jordan had to admit that Derek's theory was entirely possible. Darby didn't have a lot of time. His reasoning might be just that, hoping he could get to her in some way. Don't flatter yourself, she thought. All she wanted to know was who killed this kid. She wouldn't put it past Darby trying to smear Buck's reputation in order to get what he wanted. Jordan didn't trust Donovan either. He wouldn't go as far as being involved in a murder or a cover-up, but apparently there was very little he wouldn't do to advance his career and name recognition.

Derek had barely left when a part of the puzzle came together all of a sudden. A user by the name of TheBishop boasted about his roommate having access to Darby.

-*He's going to ask him all about his motivations.*

-*How can we know it's real?*

-*I'll give you proof. Just wait. There'll be details that weren't in the press.*

Jeffrey Bishop was hiding in plain sight. When she found herself unable to find the later conversations with the alleged proof, she called the lab to alert them of the site. She left a message for Valerie who wasn't in her office. Derek returned a moment later.

"We'll have to take those coffees to go."

"Where are we going?" he asked, checking his watch. "If I remember correctly, we're going to crash a poker game later."

"We need to have a talk with another player first. Colin's roommate was apparently active in the convos on moral decay group. Valerie isn't here yet, but I left her a message to get on it."

Derek looked a tad too doubtful for her liking.

"That's...sketchy."

"How many roommates of somebody do you think could brag with direct access to Darby? There's your connection. If anything, Bishop knows more than he told us, and I want to know what that is."

"It's worth a try," he admitted. "All right. Let's go."

They found Jeffrey Bishop at football practice, and under the curious eyes of his coach and teammates, he followed them outside of the field.

"Man, this is not a good time," he said. "Everyone here is on edge as it is. Sucks that Colin is dead, but I told you I knew next to nothing about him."

"So, you guys never talked about Jonathan Darby?"

"The serial killer? No. Why would we?"

"That's funny. Because you told your friends online he would bring you details about Darby's crimes. Did he, or did you just make that up?"

Bishop looked around himself as if to make sure no one was listening to their conversation.

"Look, that group, what people do there, it's not illegal. We're just talking about things. No one has ever met anyone who killed someone. This is considered philosophical discourse. Hypothetical, you know?"

"Then why didn't you tell us the first time we met you?" Derek asked.

Bishop shrugged. "Why would I? The person who killed Colin, that was about drugs, right? He got involved with the wrong people in the wrong neighborhood and got himself killed. The folks from that group are harmless. At least that's what he told me."

"So, you did talk about it after all?"

"Not really. I saw it on his laptop once, and he told me about it. I don't know anyone in that group in person."

"Yet you told them Colin could provide details?"

"Look." Bishop threw up his hands in surrender. "I thought it was fascinating, okay? I thought he was just a nerd, but then he was hanging out with these people, and getting the job with the lawyer who represented Darby. I mean, how close can you normally get?"

"Yeah, I see. A real opportunity." Jordan caught Derek's look at her, and she shook her head. Bishop really seemed to be the clueless one. Colin Buck...deep waters and all.

"What about those details? Did you ever go back to discuss them with the group?"

There was a knowing look on Bishop's face all of a sudden. So he understood that they were still missing parts of the conversation.

"Again, I did nothing illegal. According to Colin, he got to talk to the guy a couple of times, and he asked him. Nearly threw up afterwards too, but the people in the group thought he was cool. No one there would hurt him. You're looking in the wrong place. By the way, should I talk to a lawyer?"

"You said it yourself, you haven't done anything illegal. You also said you didn't meet with people of the group—did Colin?"

"If he did, I don't know about it. I only communicated with them online."

"Okay then."

"That's it?" He gave Jordan an incredulous look.

"Unless you have anything to add…You can go back to practice."

They went back to the car, sat for a moment. There was still time before the game at Rigley's would start.

"What a mess," Jordan said. "Unless we find proof that someone in this group wanted to kill someone, he's off the hook, and so are his disgusting friends. It's a freaking game to them. They discuss one victim at a time, extra points for details that weren't in the press. And even more points if you could get directly to the source."

"Darby might have told the truth, Donovan might be lying, but none of this helps us solve the case. There's no need for a quid pro quo."

"Not yet. We have to lean harder on Donovan."

"I'm not sure that's a good idea. He knows it's his word against Darby's. We can't ask Colin—he might have just bragged to the group about talking to him. Donovan will have a field day picking all those theories apart."

"I know, damn it. We can't prove any of it." Jordan sighed. "Let's hope we get at least lucky with Chucky Mulveney. If he knows the neighborhood that well, he might know who Colin met with that night."

Rigley's had two entrances, the main one to the bar, and a back-door on a lower level leading to a private, fenced in parking lot. They had plainclothes officers inside the building and parked close to both entrances. According to Darla's information, the poker game took place in the basement, a room from which both the stairs to the parking lot, and the main room was accessible via hallways.

Jordan and Derek took the door to the bar, spotting the officers immediately, a couple standing by the stairs leading to the lower level, and another one near the entrance. With everyone in their place, they made their way downstairs and along the corridor past the restrooms to a door that said "Private." There was a small storage room in front of another door, under which a small strip of light could be seen. The other officers were just steps away from the entrance behind it.

Jordan opened the door to a startled-looking group of people sitting around a table, five men, one woman. "Sorry, folks. We need to chat with Mr. Mulveney, that's all. And please, don't try anything funny. The place is surrounded."

"What do you want?" Mulveney asked, looking her up and down with a condescending smile. "You got a warrant? My friends and I were enjoying a game. That's not illegal, is it?"

"I'd prefer it if you came with us. We could use your expertise...and word is out that since Ryder's been busted, you're the man to go to."

"Is that so? Who told you?"

"It's not important, but if you can help us, this could be a two-way conversation."

"The way I see it, you're trespassing on private property. I'd like to see that warrant if you have one, otherwise *I'd prefer* if you leave right—"

Abruptly, the woman jumped to her feet and ran. Two of the men stared after her slack jawed. A third one pulled a gun and shot at the ceiling light, plunging the room into darkness.

It had been another busy day. Ellie was well aware of Casey's sideways looks, but she couldn't help it. She liked a tight schedule. She liked not having to obsess about the future, which chances to take, something she'd done for the better part of her life.

She was a good cop. Her colleagues said so. Her parents would have been so proud of her. She knew Jordan was proud of her. That mattered.

The call came in less than fifteen minutes before the end of her shift, a massive car accident involving a truck and two other vehicles. She and Casey were only two blocks away, and sirens blaring, they sped towards the scene a moment later.

The accident had happened at an intersection. An ambulance was already on the scene, two others arriving.

Casey and Ellie learned that the truck driver had walked away with a few bruises and cuts. The man in one of the other cars was conscious but bleeding from a head wound. Paramedics were able to open the door on his side and started to tend to him. Ellie's heart lurched into her throat when she saw the woman in the driver's seat of the third car, a toddler buckled into car seat in the back, crying. The woman's airbag had deployed. She didn't move. One of the windows in the back was cracked, but not completely broken.

Ellie tried the driver's door which didn't budge. The door in the back gave. A broken fingernail or two were a small price to pay. The girl and her mother—Ellie assumed—needed to go to the hospital as soon as possible.

"Don't worry, sweetie, we'll get you out of here in no time."

She reached inside to remove the girl's seatbelt which came off after some resistance. So far so good.

"What's your name?" she asked, to no avail. There were no visible injuries. A paramedic had come up behind her, and she carefully picked up the girl and handed her to him.

"Ellie!"

She turned to Casey, for a split-second wondering why her friend had gotten pale—the she smelled it too.

"Damn it, no!"

"Come on. We have to get out of here."

"No way."

Ellie tore herself away from Casey's grip.

"Ellie, don't be stupid! This thing is going to blow! You need to get away from the car now."

"I'm not going to let that girl be an orphan," Ellie muttered to herself as Casey herded everyone on the scene to a safe area.

Ellie reached inside the car, and with a bit of wiggling, she managed to get the seat all the way down. The woman moaned in pain. There was some blood on her leg, but to Ellie's relief she wasn't stuck. Ellie's mind was completely blank as to the danger, even as she saw the flame licking at metal. She managed to get the woman out and drag her a few feet before Casey and another paramedic came to her help.

"Have you lost your freaking—"

The rest of Casey's words were lost in a deafening bang.

Chapter Eight

M ulveney's room for negotiation was shrinking rapidly, but their back-up had reacted right away. Flashlights illuminated the room within seconds to reveal that the only damage done was the overhead lamp. There was shattered glass everywhere—and now they had a reason to bring in every one of them. Officer Libby Marshall had caught up with the fleeing woman who had cocaine on her. The man who had shot at the lamp, Ronnie Dexter, had no registration for his weapon.

All in all, it was shaping up to be a successful evening by the time they were back at the department.

"The thing is, we can still help you," Jordan said as she perched on the edge of the table in the interrogation room. "You know your neighborhood, right? The regulars, the ones that are out of place. You'd know if someone didn't belong—or if someone was trespassing onto your territory."

"You are giving me a lot of credit, lady."

"Credit where credit is due." She shrugged. "I'm not looking to trick you. I want to know why a college kid was shot a few feet away from where a neighbor saw you and your boys hang out. We think it's a deal gone wrong. If there was an amateur involved, maybe they were on your radar too."

"It's a good story," he said. "I'm just not sure how I can help you. I don't deal. If the kid was looking for some entertainment, I wouldn't know to help him."

"Unless he wanted to play poker," she said sarcastically.

"Oh, don't mind Ronnie. He has a nervous trigger finger."

"What about Alicia Jones? You didn't provide her with the cocaine?"

"No, I didn't. Sorry. Can I call my lawyer now?"

"You know, much of this could go away if you could give us a few ideas as to whom Mr. Buck might have met with. There's been a vacuum since Ryder was busted. Somehow, I don't think everyone would be happy just letting you take over."

He gave a dramatic sigh. "I'd like to confer with my lawyer first, but I might have something for you."

"Might is not good enough."

"All right. Let me put it this way. There has been some tourism in the area lately. Alicia says there was a guy asking her all kinds of weird questions, like did she go to the All Colors." He shook his head, laughing. "As if that's her kind of scene."

Jordan felt the blood drain from her face. At the All Colors, a place where everyone could hook up with anyone, Darby had been stalking some of his victims.

"We will talk to Alicia, and it will be lucky for both of you if she can make an ID."

"Yeah, well, you do that. Can I make that call now?"

⌘

Ellie's ears were ringing. She stared in shock at the destroyed vehicle, the flames shooting up in the sky where she had been standing minutes ago. The woman was unconscious, but stable in the back of the ambulance that was leaving for the hospital.

"Officer. Please come with me?" a soft voice insisted, and she followed the paramedic. Casey was right behind them.

"You saved that woman's life," she said. Ellie thought it sounded a tad admonishing, but maybe she was in shock too. "Ellie."

"Yes, what?"

"Should I call someone for you? Jordan?"

"Oh, no, I'm fine." She might have scraped her knees when they dove for cover. "Don't call her. I'll meet her at the station. She'll just worry for nothing." She was glad to sit down though. "Now that you're asking, I think I'm kind of dizzy."

"I'm not surprised," the paramedic said. "Let's get you checked out first."

Casey laid her hand on the small of her back. "I'll come with you."

Ellie closed her eyes for a moment, trying to piece together the past few minutes in her mind. "She'll be okay? Both the mom and the child?"

"Yes. You did something very brave...that could have gotten you killed."

Ellie winced, unhappy with Casey's words. She had the feeling that she was going to hear a variation of them more often—but there was no way she could have done anything differently.

❦

Jordan had just sat down in the room where Derek was interviewing Alicia Jones when Detective Doss knocked on the door.

"Jordan, do you have a moment?" she asked.

"Can it wait a minute?"

"It's about Ellie," Doss said. Jordan was on her feet in an instant.

"She's okay," Maria Doss added once they were outside a room. "She'll be waiting for you in the break room when you're done here."

"Okay…What *aren't* you telling me?"

"I don't know all the details, but they were called to the scene of a car crash. One of the cars caught fire. Ellie got the driver out before it blew, and she's okay."

For a split second, the world tilted, but Jordan held on to the word "okay." Maria sounded reasonably calm, which was an immeasurable relief.

"You wouldn't come here though if there wasn't any bad news."

"It was close," Maria said. "Everyone was advised not to go near the vehicle. Lyons tried to stop her."

"And she would have none of it." There was nothing more Jordan wanted at this moment than convince herself that Ellie was okay. "Look, I can't leave here right now, but could you tell her to wait for me?"

"You don't want to take a few minutes…?" Maria's incredulous gaze spoke volumes.

"It won't be long."

The truth was she couldn't. If Maria said Ellie was okay, Jordan trusted her, but that didn't mean her stomach wasn't in knots. If she went there right now, she might lose it, and that wouldn't help either of them. If she took a little time to breathe, get those images out of her head, she'd be able to be supportive, tell Ellie how proud she was of her instead of shaking her for disobeying a direct order.

"Are you sure?"

"Go already, get her a coffee, okay? I'll be wrapping things up here."

She went back into the room without waiting for an answer.

"All right, Ms. Jones. I don't have a lot of time. Mr. Mulveney tells me an acquaintance of yours asked about the All Colors. It would be very helpful for both of us if you could describe him to us."

"I'll try," Alicia Jones said timidly. "He called himself The Knight. Some sort of gamer, I assumed. He was really good-looking too."

⁂

By the time Jordan was ready to leave, the unsettling mixture of anxiety and frustration hadn't worn off much. She blamed most of it on Darby, and the bizarre development that they might be looking for a serial killer fan club whose member names were chess pieces. Then there was the fact that Ellie had saved a woman from a burning car, against everyone's judgment.

The woman was alive.

This was an act for bravery.

It meant she could have lost Ellie today. That's where the anxiety came in.

She went to her desk, turned off her computer and finally headed for the break room.

"Hey," she said softly. "I'm sorry, I had to finish this up first."

Ellie turned to her, to Jordan's relief looking unharmed. She held up scraped palms. "I guess you heard. That's about it, so please, don't freak out."

Jordan walked farther into the room and sat next to her, re-sisting the urge to hold her head in her hands. Ellie was probably the one with the legitimate headache.

"You're not freaking out, right? I'm fine."

"I'm okay. You're a hero." Jordan leaned in to kiss her gently. "You hear okay?"

"Now I do, yes. Wow. It was crazy."

"I can imagine. You're ready to go home?"

"Yes. You?"

"Absolutely. We're going to have an early start tomorrow, so I guess I'm inviting myself over."

They had a possible ID on The Knight, the good-looking guy Bishop had described as the one who'd been asking for Buck. There had been no one by that name in the "talks on moral decay" group. Either he didn't know him, or he had lied to them again. Either way, they were going to find out tomorrow.

Later that night, when Ellie was asleep in her arms, Jordan almost resented her for her ability to have a break from today's events—even if it was just the adrenaline high wearing off. Ellie hadn't volunteered much information besides the obvious. They had talked about the upcoming house viewing. Jordan didn't feel much like sharing either, because then they'd have to talk about groups that glorified serial murderers, and one in particular that did so with Darby.

The silver lining in all this was the house viewing which could bring them closer to a home of their own soon. She was equally looking forward to the end of the trial which would take a huge weight off of Ariel's shoulders.

She was still mad at Ellie for risking her life to save another, her conflicting emotions luring her onto a trip down memory lane...

The ringing of the phone, what seemed only minutes after she'd fallen asleep, left Jordan disoriented for a moment. Beside her, Bethany was stirring, muttering an expletive. Understandable—Jordan had missed her earlier message that she was going to be home tonight, so she'd spent the evening with friends at the Code 7. They didn't have much time to talk, which was clearly Jordan's fault, something that had become eerily familiar.

"Carpenter," she said after accepting the call, pushing back the sheets. A call at this time of night meant that sleep was over.

"Hey, Jordan. I'm at the hospital." Derek Henderson, her partner, sounded stressed.

"What? Why?"

"An officer from our precinct. You know her. Harding. She was beaten badly."

"Oh my God. When?"

Bethany was fully awake now, too, studying Jordan as she gathered her clothes, dressing quickly. There was no judgment in her gaze. The urgency of a call like that, she could understand. It was one of the few subjects between them that wouldn't cause an argument, never had.

"Not long ago," Derek said. "A resident called 911, the perp got away. A few of us came here...We're waiting for the doctor."

"I'll be there in a few."

"One of our colleagues was assaulted," she told Bethany. "I have to go to the hospital."

"Sure. How bad is it?"

"We don't know yet."

An icy chill ran down Jordan's spine, a sliver of guilt mixed in with all the other emotions she'd have if it was any other colleague.

Harding. Ellie. She'd seen her at roll call, and at the Code 7 a few times, a short blonde, pretty, usually hanging out with her friends...giving Jordan the eye from across the room.

She'd have to lie if she said it wasn't flattering...or tempting, which definitely made her the bad person once more. She couldn't go down that road again. The last time, she had begged Bethany to take her back, overly dramatic, as if she'd be broke and homeless without her. The memory was still laden with shame.

None of this mattered, because this wasn't about Jordan.

Someone had beaten the young officer badly enough to put her in the hospital.

Someone familiar? Revenge? An angry ex? They were going to find out. Officially, or unofficially, every cop in the city was on the case now.

That sounded much better in her head. She might have mis-interpreted the signs after all, and either way, it didn't matter. Jordan was trying to get her life together, to keep her relationship with Bethany intact and on track.

Nevertheless, she acknowledged a moment of utter, unadul-terated fear. She caught herself praying, something that didn't happen very often. Jordan didn't think anyone would blame her at this moment.

⁂

Jordan didn't know much about Ellie Harding, but she noticed that there was no family, blood relatives in any case, which wasn't always the best definition of family anyway. She recognized Ellie's peers from the bar, other officers, McCarthy, Baker, Marshall. McCarthy—Kate—looked like she'd been crying.

"She'll be okay," Derek came up beside her, holding a steaming paper cup of coffee out to her. "She's going to be in pain though, when she wakes up," he explained to both Kate and Jordan.

"We got a good description?"

He shrugged. "It was dark. 911 caller said he wore dark clothes and a mask. Son of a bitch tried to take her."

"Okay, hang on." Reality had taken a sharp turn to much worse—or was she overreacting? "You think it could be the same guy—?"It couldn't be. If he had tried to take another woman already, it meant he was escalating. Not having succeeded would make him angry, act sooner...

"We'll have to wait for her to wake up," Derek reminded her. "Now's not the time to make assumptions."

76

He didn't mean to be patronizing, just stating the obvious. Jordan ascertained that he was probably right.

"I want to see her."

"She's asleep. There's nothing we can get out of her now..." Derek let his sentence trail off, looking somewhere between concerned and alarmed as it dawned on him that Jordan wasn't talking about Harding's statement. She felt the same.

She shook her head and left in search of the doctor.

To her relief, the woman didn't even question her request.

"Just for a moment, please, okay? She needs her rest now."

A few seconds later, Jordan stood next to the hospital bed, watching Ellie Harding, still, silent, her face bruised as the rest of her body surely was, a bandage on her temple.

Ellie was hardly ever this silent, always quick with a smile, and from what little Jordan had heard about her, she had a great career ahead. Dedicated, smart.

Someone had tried to put a stop to it—someone random or familiar?

She reached out to take Ellie's hand in hers, unsure why she was doing it—why she was the one to do it—but feeling strangely comforted by the contact.

"Hang in there," she whispered. "You're going to be okay." Despite the predictable period of pain medication, physical therapy and nightmares.

Spooked by her own reaction, she left the room abruptly. They had a job to do. Maybe, Bethany would forgive her for the previous night and meet her for a quick breakfast somewhere. She could only hope.

Her prayers had come true—she hadn't lost Ellie, that time, and this time. Her attacker had been caught, and Jordan had been able to leave behind a relationship that made neither her nor Bethany happy any longer. It was time to look ahead—especially since she had to admit that in Ellie's situation, she would have done the same. She couldn't shake the sense of fear, and anger.

Jordan scooted closer to her and finally managed to slip into sleep as well. Her conflicting emotions followed, creating dark and disturbing dreams.

What happened the next morning wasn't a usual occurrence for Ellie: Near the entrance of the station, a reporter was waiting for her.

"Officer Harding, would you have a few minutes for me? You saved the woman from a burning car yesterday, going against your superior's orders, risking your own life..."

The expression on Jordan's face told Ellie that they were still going to have that conversation. "I have to go," Jordan said. "I'll see you later."

Ellie turned to the reporter. "Look, there's not much I can tell you. It's my job. It was risky, but it turned out okay, and I'm glad we could save a life."

"Have you talked to Rita Williamson since the incident?"

"No, there was no time. Actually, I don't have a lot of time now, I'm sorry, Ms..."

"Allen. That's no problem. Thank you for your time."

"That was weird," Ellie said to herself as she opened the door.

"Get used to it," Derek Henderson, who had come in behind her, said. "Rita Williamson, the name rings a bell, no? She owns five restaurants in the city. Besides, that was amazing. You deserve the credit."

"Come on," Ellie said, uncomfortable with the praise, though she wished it could have come from Jordan instead.

Jordan, however, was still working out things on her own. It was something Ellie was still getting used to.

Casey had the same disapproving look on her face. "You're not even taking a half day?"

"Because I scraped my knees and hands? Come on. No one would."

Fortunately, Casey left the subject alone after that, and they went about their day, which was surprisingly quiet after the past ones. Truth be told, Ellie felt relieved. She hadn't yet completely processed yesterday's events.

She got a distraction, if not a welcome one, when she ran into Derek later that day. Jordan was nowhere to be seen.

"You look really happy," she said, half-joking.

"That's because I am. We just picked up a human chess piece who has a crush on Darby, and he's happy to talk about it. That means there is no reason we should go back and talk to that asshole, and he can die already."

Ellie nodded, wondering how she could get more information out of him without revealing that Jordan hadn't spoken to her about this at all. When had they seen Darby? And why would Jordan keep it from her?

"Yeah, I don't think anyone will shed a tear. So, you're about to wrap things up? This serial killer fan, he killed Colin Buck?"

"It looks that way."

"Darby was just bragging to get attention again."

"Yeah. Excuse me now? I have to go back."

"Sure."

Ellie stood in front of the vending machine, sighing at her reflection in the glass. It would all be better sometime soon. She had never wished for anyone's death before, but there was no denying the world would be a better place without Jonathan Darby in it.

Chapter Nine

The Knight, a man by the name of Marcus Holmes, admitted to meeting Colin Buck that night, claiming that a fight with Buck got out of control when he refused to pay for the drugs he'd bought. Holmes killed him in self-defense.

"Really? You were the one with the gun, and you felt your life was threatened?" Esposito asked sarcastically.

"You didn't find his? You really think he'd come to this place unarmed?"

Jordan suppressed a sigh knowing they'd have to get back to that.

Holmes also confirmed hanging out at the All Colors from time to time. He denied that the group revered Darby online or in person.

"Hey, we're not sick. We weren't planning to kill anyone, ever. This was about philosophy."

"It has become pretty real, don't you think?"

Secretly, Jordan found it a relief that even criminals drew the line somewhere.

"Well, whatever you think, Detective, you're wrong. This was a one-time thing I did for a friend, and I freaked. I'm sorry Colin is dead. I didn't mean for that to happen. You have to believe me."

"A jury will decide on that," she said. Jordan doubted that Buck had brought a gun to the meeting as well, and she didn't believe Holmes' remorse was more than an act, but he didn't budge.

The week was finally over. They had talked to Ariel on the phone, and to Ms. Sherman, and fortunately she confirmed that things were quiet at the home. Now, she and Ellie had a rather busy weekend ahead, with the house viewing in the morning, and a dinner at Jack and Pauline's on Saturday night.

With Holmes in custody, she hoped they could put the subject of Darby behind them once and for all, which, in Jordan's terms, meant to never bring it up again.

Andrea Cox had chosen a charming bungalow-style home to show them. It was within walking distance to many cafés and restaurants, only a fifteen-minute drive to work. So far, so good.

"This one is under your budget," Cox told them. "If you're not afraid to do a little work, then this could be perfect for you."

Ellie looked hesitant. "What kind of work exactly, and what do you mean by 'a little'?"

"If you prefer an open concept, you might want to bring down a wall...I was able to take a look at the plans, and it would be entirely possible."

Ellie gave her a questioning look, and Jordan shrugged. That didn't sound too dire. Her family might be carpenters in name only, but she knew Jack had done a number of projects in the home she'd grown up in, and he'd taught her some tricks. He'd certainly be willing to help, too.

"I like it already," Ellie said. "I hope we can manage the inside as well."

The living room, dining room and a half bath were in good shape. They both winced a bit at the state of the kitchen that seemed to stem from another area altogether.

"The owners did some updates...obviously not everywhere," Andrea explained.

"Okay. So far, the wall is coming down, and the kitchen is a gut job." Jordan hadn't meant for it to sound so sarcastic. Her tone hadn't gone unnoticed with Ellie, who gave her a quick, surprised sideways look.

"I don't know, maybe we could live with it for a while?" she chimed in. "It's not like we cook all the time."

"We can afford it. I'd like to see something from the present in here."

"You're right. Let's see the rest."

There were a couple of other bedrooms, plus a master suite that could use a little TLC as well, and a huge space underneath the roof. The house needed work, no doubt, but it was something they could grow into. A big difference from the place where Bethany had been happy to make most of the decisions, or the house she had bought just to get away from it all. The street was fairly quiet even though it wasn't far from a more lively area, and from the attic, they had seen a good-sized backyard.

"I don't know," Ellie said. "I love it, I really do, but...I think I'd like to see one more."

"Funny how it took you only seconds to make a decision when your life was at stake."

Ellie cast an uncertain look at where Andrea Cox was following a few feet behind.

"I don't really want to have that conversation right now."

"Fine, when are we going to have that conversation about how you nearly died?"

It wasn't until she saw Ellie and Andrea flinch that Jordan realized she'd raised her voice.

"Come on. Stop it! I thought we were over this, you telling me how to do my job."

"I can wait outside if you want to—"

"No." Jordan didn't wait for her to finish her sentence, and the agent caught the hint and quietly went back downstairs. "That's not what it's about. There's taking risks, and then there's getting yourself killed. Thank God, everything worked out for you and the woman this time. You were damn lucky. There's no way you could have assessed the situation so quickly. What if her injuries had been more severe? The car would have blown up just the same."

Ellie shook her head in exasperation. "But her injuries weren't more severe, and I could get her out. We're both alive and okay, and so is her young daughter by the way. Please, stop for a minute, and don't try to tell me you wouldn't have done the same thing. You were evacuating the area around the *Code 7* minutes before the blast. And if we really want to go there, why didn't you call for backup when you found Darby's hidden basement?"

"Because Judy Lawrence didn't have that much time!" Jordan realized a moment too late that the trap had snapped shut, or that's how it felt to her.

"Yes. Think about that for a moment. I think I'll go home for a bit. It's a nice house. I need to sleep on it first."

Ellie spun on her heels and hastened down the steps.

"Wait! Are you coming to dinner at my parents' later?"

"I'll think about it."

Andrea Cox was waiting for Jordan downstairs, giving her a sympathetic look at the sound of the car's engine.

"I can give you a ride," she said.

"Thank you. That would be great."

Andrea Cox drove away by herself when she and Jordan realized that Ellie hadn't left, but was waiting in the car.

"I'm sorry," they both said at the same time when Jordan sat inside. "I mean it," Ellie continued. "I didn't plan to go off on you about all the times I was scared for you."

"Same here."

"Knowing that you went to see Darby didn't help."

"I can imagine." Jordan leaned back into her seat with a sigh. "I didn't actually see him. That was his plan, but there's no need now. We have a confession."

"Yeah, Derek told me. Well, I kind of tricked him into telling me. It's not his fault."

Jordan took her hand, squeezing it lightly. "I am freaked out, I'll admit it. I'm going to need a moment." She had read all the reports, including Ellie's. She couldn't spend any more time being angry at her, but the images those words evoked still disturbed her. Too many close calls, in a short period of time. She couldn't help lingering on those events and was once more grateful that Ellie was the complete opposite. Forward. With Ellie, it was always forward.

"Yeah." Ellie's expression turned solemn. "For a reason. It freaked me out, too, but there was a chance, and I took it. Everyone came out of it okay."

"I came to see you in the hospital the other time."

The words were out of her mouth before she could contemplate whether or not it would be a good idea to say them. Jordan could tell that Ellie wasn't making the connection.

"After I got kidnapped? I remember—"

"No, the other time. When you were attacked. Derek called me, and I went in to see you."

"Oh. Okay." Ellie didn't seem to know what to say to that, or why Jordan was even bringing it up at this moment.

After all, Jordan was with Bethany at the time, foolishly thinking they could fix their relationship. There had been something that was stronger—more meaningful, and she'd been scared of losing it, right from the start.

"They let you into the room?"

"It wasn't that hard."

Ellie pondered this new information for a few seconds. "Why did you do it? I mean…You barely knew me."

"I didn't really admit it until later. I had noticed you, and I…wanted you. Before that night, even. I guess what I'm trying to say is, I didn't mean to go off on you like I did. I can't lose you."

That was the heart of the matter, the whole truth. Ellie held on to her hand as her eyes welled up.

"You apologized already. That's good enough for me."

"Yeah, well, you should know the whole story."

"Thank you. I understand what you want to say."

That was the best part of their relationship—they might disagree on some subjects, favor a different approach, but they truly understood each other. It had helped them through the rockier times, and it would serve them in everything that lay ahead.

"I love you."

"I love you too," Ellie said firmly. "And I want you to relax and enjoy tonight. We earned it."

She'd give it a try, even if Jordan was at times still struggling with the idea that she might deserve a person like Ellie in her life.

"What are we going to do about the house?" Ellie asked after a few seconds of silence. "It's going to need some work, but I like it. We could make it our own."

Jordan agreed. "It's exactly where we want to be. It has everything we want."

"So let's do it. I promise you I'll be as careful as I can. I won't leave you hanging with the mortgage—and I expect the same from you."

"Deal," Jordan said and pulled her close for a kiss.

⁕

They had barely made it to Ellie's apartment when Kathryn called.

"Jordan. I was wondering if you could meet me for lunch. I know it's on short notice, but...I'd like to see you if that's okay."

"Are you all right?" Her birthmother had been to the hospital for tests recently, and as expected, she was not in excellent health. Worrying about her still led to a multitude of mixed emotions.

"Yes, I'd just like to see you."

She could say no. It was her right to draw lines—the shrink had said so. Jordan had also begun to harbor a morbid curiosity regarding Kathryn, so she had only herself to blame.

"I'm at Ellie's now. I don't have long, but I could meet you at Max's for an hour or so." There was a pause long enough to turn awkward. "Or we could do it another day."

"No, that's fine. I'll be there."

"You want me to come with you?" Ellie asked. Her question had merit. It was debatable how well Jordan had handled prior meetings with Kathryn. On the other hand, she knew what to expect now. She had opened that door and intended to keep it open as long as Kathryn appeared to be trustworthy. This was mostly for Jordan's benefit—again, it was the shrink's opinion, but Ellie, Jack and Pauline shared it.

"I'll be fine. I'll see you later at Jack and Pauline's?"

"Yes. Have a good time. I'm glad you're going."

"Yeah, well, I'll tell you all about it later."

Max's bistro was reasonably priced. Jordan had to admit it hadn't been her first consideration, but when she saw Kathryn walk in, looking around, she felt somewhat guilty. Which wasn't fair—whatever financial troubles she and Jim might be in these days, Jordan had nothing to do with it. It wasn't up to her to fix things for them. Going as far as she had was showing of a lot of good will already, wasn't it?

"It's good to see you." Kathryn smiled, using the moment for a quick hug. She had already figured out that she had to take her chances.

"You too. What's the matter?"

"Oh, nothing special," Kathryn said as she sat down, and then quickly corrected herself. "What am I saying, that's stupid. Seeing you is always special to me. It's a nice place."

"Yeah, I came here with my partner once. They opened not long ago." Jordan let her words trail off, running out of subjects for small talk.

"How are you?" Kathryn asked.

"Good. Busy," Jordan said vaguely, and then she blurted out, "Ellie and I are buying a house. So yes, things are good."

"It's serious, then. That's wonderful."

She had to stop finding a challenge in every word, Jordan reflected. "Yes, it is. I'll be closer to the city."

After their orders had arrived, a soup for Kathryn, and a salad for Jordan, she asked, "Do you want to get married?"

Funny how that question came as absolutely no surprise. Jordan felt herself smile, some of the tension that was always present in Kathryn's company, vanishing.

"I haven't asked her yet, but I plan to, yes."

"I'm so happy for you. You deserve all of this, and more."

"Come on."

"It's true, and it means so much to me that I can be around this time. I also wanted to give you this." Kathryn took a couple of twenties out of her wallet. Jordan couldn't help notice that they were the only bills in it, and that the wallet was about to fall apart. "I know it's not all, but I'm pretty sure I can give you the rest next time. Thank you."

Jordan pushed the bills back towards her. "I didn't mean for you to give it back. You needed those meds. It's fine."

"Please." Kathryn had very well understood the message between the lines, something closer to *I never expected you to even try.*

Jordan felt herself blush.

"All right. Sure. Let me pay for lunch, then."

"If you insist. Look, if that's all right with both of you, Ellie could come along sometime. I'd love to get to know her too."

"I'll ask her," Jordan said, though she was deeply unsure of how she felt about this idea. Ellie would probably welcome it. Just like that, Kathryn would make herself at home in their lives. It seemed too quick, too easy. On the other hand, they didn't have an endless amount of time.

"Thank you. Thank you so much." Kathryn took her hands, and Jordan had a hard time resisting the urge to pull back. There was a necessity for boundaries in their careful negotiations. Kathryn was testing them.

"You're welcome."

They heard the sound of a vibrating cell phone. Jordan checked hers only to realize that the call was for Kathryn. "Excuse me?" she said and answered.

An older model, Jordan realized and chided herself instantly. It wasn't up to her or anyone else to judge. Kathryn quickly ended a call.

"That was Jim, he just came back. I guess I have to go too—thank you for seeing me. It means more than you can ever imagine."

After she had left, Jordan took a moment to reflect on their conversation. Her summary of it wasn't good. How was it possible that she still felt the need to impress Kathryn—or maybe brag about what she'd become in spite of her incompetent birthparents? The house would probably be a go, but whatever had possessed her to talk about marriage before she'd told Jack and Pauline, or more importantly, raised the question with Ellie?

If they were going to make plans, would Kathryn expect to be invited, even though she'd had no interest in Jordan's life in the past twenty years or so?

She finally left the bistro and drove all the way back to her house to change, needing the commute to clear her mind.

Marriage, did it matter for the two of them? What would it change? It hadn't been enough for Jim and Kathryn to create two responsible human beings. Kathryn had cheated on Jim.

However, that didn't mean she had to repeat those mistakes. She and Ellie could do better. They already had. She could possibly delay the conversation on wedding invitations a little while longer.

Chapter Ten

W hen Jordan arrived at her parents', she wasn't hungry, but she did accept the glass of wine that Pauline handed her in the kitchen. Jack was on the phone in the office.

"He might have a little surprise," Pauline said with a wink. "But let's talk about you. You solved the murder of that college kid—I read about it in the newspaper. I also read about Ellie. You have much to celebrate. Does she have any idea when she can get a detective job?"

Jordan decided to skip the more complicated parts of the past week, the possible connection to a dying serial killer, or the way she'd gone off on Ellie for doing something incredibly brave.

"It's been...a busy time. We did manage to see a house this morning, though...and we really love it."

"That's amazing. If you need any work done, Jack can help you, you know? It's not as far out as where you live now? It always makes me uneasy to think of..." Pauline let her words trail off, not revealing if the location, or how that house sale originated, was her major concern. "I'm so happy for you. This is a big step."

"Yeah." Jordan let herself be embraced, the gesture feeling less awkward than it had with Kathryn, of course, but she was still questioning her actions—and words. "I saw Kathryn too."

"You did?" Pauline made a small pause as if to let the timing of this encounter sink in. However, she made up her mind quickly. "That's good. Don't get me wrong, I know you're careful, and I think you have every reason. But if she's honest, and you can have a relationship now, it's not a bad thing."

Jordan took a sip of her wine. "I'm so sorry."

"About what?"

"I told her first...She asked if I wanted to marry Ellie. I said yes, and...it's strange to share that with her. I should have told you first."

"Well, Ellie is the one you should consult first, but I have no doubt whatsoever that she'll say yes. I can't wait! A wedding. I so look forward to that."

"Who's getting married?" Jack asked from the doorway. "Wait..."

While Jordan appreciated everyone's enthusiasm, the hugging was getting a bit much.

"I love you, but please, slow down, both of you. Nothing's planned yet. Ellie doesn't even know. Let's please forget about it until it's a done deal?"

Pauline and Jack shared an amused look. The doorbell rang.

"Don't tell her, okay?"

"Not a word," Jack promised.

For a moment, Jordan remembered what it had been like when she'd wondered if something she'd achieved would make her birthparents proud—and then felt guilty about it, because she had it so much better with Jack and Pauline, and their opinions were the only ones that counted now.

Ariel, whatever her path was, would likely grow up with the same dilemma...unless someone prepared her for it.

When they sat down for dinner, she remembered what Pauline had told her earlier.

"Pauline said you had a surprise?"

"That's right. I wanted to wait until Ellie was here. You might have heard that the property where the *Code 7* stood is for sale. I'm thinking about buying it to rebuild."

"You want to run a bar?" Jordan asked, baffled.

"I have a friend who would get in on it. I know many of you miss the place, and this is a chance to bring back some of the memories. We could call it *Carpenter's*."

"Oh my God, Jack, no."

The words were out before she realized Jack was probably not one hundred percent serious, about the name, anyway. Ellie's amusement, Jordan was sure, had another reason. They had some special memories of the place indeed, one of which they could never share with anyone else.

She had to admit the thought was intriguing.

"Speaking of restaurants," Ellie said. "Mrs. Williamson called me. We got an invitation to *Le Luxembourg*."

"That's amazing," Pauline said.

"Yeah, it is. I think an appetizer plate is the price of our weekly budget for eating out."

When Jordan saw Ellie's grateful smile, Jordan knew it was the right thing to keep the tone light, if only for a few hours with Jack and Pauline. She, too, wanted to forget for a while what Ellie had done to receive such an invitation from one of the richest women in the city.

❦

Monday mid-morning, Jordan took a quick coffee break, her thoughts drifting to wedding plans and squeezing in meeting Ariel before the trial. She was catching up on her paperwork when Detective Doss came hastening into the room.

"Did you hear?"

"No. What are you talking about?"

"It's on the news now. A woman walked into traffic near the mall. We know her. Joy Anne Deane."

"She's one of Daniel's wives?" Jordan shuddered at the memory. They had to question everyone living on the compound, but not all women had been aware of the crimes committed, either because they weren't privy, or they had grown into those structures not even knowing their rights. Jordan remembered her now, wearing the dress that the brothers running the cult had made mandatory for women and girls.

"Yes. From what I know, she's hanging in there. I thought you might want to come."

"Sure. Let's go."

"She's eighteen, recently had a miscarriage." Maria shuddered. "Those bastards. It's about time they face some consequences. They had multiple wives younger than that."

She was mostly voicing her own disbelief, knowing that Jordan had written some of those reports, read all of them. The press had been focused on how one of the cult members had been a cold-blooded murderer, his actions covered up by the family patriarch. In the screaming headlines, the day-to-day abuse those women and girls had been subjected to, had sometimes gotten lost.

Joy Anne would have been called to testify, as she had not been legally married to Daniel Deane and therefore didn't have a choice.

The news was devastating. It would be for the other women, and it surely would be for Ariel who was so much braver than any girl her age should need to be.

"I can't believe this is all over the news already? With the trial coming up, someone should have put a lid on it." Jordan had to admit it was somewhat selfish. There was no way Joseph would be able to weasel out of the charges. For the other men, it was on a case-by-case basis. An illegal "marriage" with a minor would make a good point for the prosecution, but they had to prove that they had been taking place, and that the Deane men had been responsible. They had Agent Lilah Strickland's testimony, and the book written by Jennifer Beaumont, who had been murdered by one of the cult members, but they hadn't witnessed those weddings in person.

Too much hinged on the testimony of Ariel, and the less loyal women, who would no doubt be painted as traitors. Ariel was one of the few who had not acted hostile towards the police. She and her mother, Joseph's last victim, had wanted out, planned their escape for a long time.

"You think the girl is going to go through with the testimony? She's not going to crack?" Maria Doss asked.

"No," Jordan said with conviction. "Ariel is tough. She knows wrong from right too."

Did Joy Anne? Had somebody tried to stop her from telling the truth, or had the idea of losing her family, if she testified, been too much?

Ariel was grieving her mother, and she had been fairly cavalier about the fact that her father didn't want her. Given the charges against him, she was probably right.

What if she, too, became overwhelmed with the reality of her situation, the tug of war between loyalty and truth?

Jordan knew all too well how that felt, and how it had impacted her life. The thought of Ariel faced with that same decision sent an icy chill down her spine.

❧

Ellie was sure that Ariel was on Jordan's mind too as she found her in the ER waiting room.

"There were a handful of witnesses," she told her. "All say the same—she walked right into traffic. No one pushed her."

"That didn't mean no one threatened her," Jordan said. "She never wanted to testify in the first place, but since she's not the legal wife, she would have to."

"You think one of the lawyers got to her?"

"It's possible—or even one of the other women. It's terrible to even think about it, but you can't keep up a system like that for so long without using the people in it against one another. If a lawyer contacted her, or one of the brothers, it would be easier to trace. I'm sure the women talk amongst themselves now, their future. Some have been loyal all their lives—it would be hard to change that."

"You think there will be more incidents?" Ellie was aware that her question painted a dark picture.

"I don't know. It's possible. Even if Joy Anne made that decision for herself only, it will send shockwaves through their community. Other women might be discouraged from speaking out."

"We need to talk to Ariel."

Jordan nodded. "I know. The press will go after her harder."

"I wish we could have done more, but people had their cell phones out seconds after it happened. Could we justify a safe house? I know Mary Sherman is doing her best with all the girls, but I'm not sure she has the resources to protect Ariel."

"I'll talk to the lieutenant, and Valerie, see what we can do. Will you go see her? I'll call you when I know more."

"Sure. I'm on my way."

<hr>

When she arrived at the group home, Ellie went straight to Mary Sherman's office.

"I guess you're here about the other girl. That's terrible."

"Yes. We want to make sure that Ariel is protected all the way to the trial, and afterwards."

"You're going to take her out of here?" Sherman looked doubtful. "We had no problems with her family. Sad as it is, I believe they don't consider her one of their own anymore."

"Joy Anne Deane was set to testify as well. We can't take any chances. I am waiting for a call from Detective Carpenter, but I'd like to talk to Ariel, inform her about the next steps."

"Sure, why don't we go upstairs and get her?"

The doorbell rang, and Sherman excused herself. "I'll be right back."

A moment later, Ellie heard a familiar voice. She would have liked more time to prepare Ariel. On the bright side, if Valerie Esposito was here already, it meant that things were moving fast. She stepped outside Sherman's office to greet the A.D.A.

"Jordan talked to you about the safehouse?"

"Yes. It's important we don't waste any time on this. We still don't know what triggered this, and regardless, we don't want the press or anyone to find out where she is right now."

Sherman shook her head. "I told Officer Harding already that we didn't have any problems, with the press or members of the family."

"Yeah, well, those problems could easily arise now," Esposito said. "Ariel is coming with us."

"Can I have a minute with her first?" Ellie asked.

"I don't have a problem with that but make it quick."

"Thank you."

She and Mary Sherman went up the stairs to Ariel's room. Sherman knocked. "Ariel? Officer Harding is here for you."

Detective, Ellie corrected in her mind, even though that had no bearing on the situation. She just had to remind herself sometimes.

There was no response.

"Ariel?" Sherman opened the door. Ellie followed her into the room—no Ariel. The window stood open, curtains wafting in the cold air.

"Damn it, Ariel, no."

Ellie felt the same. She imagined this wasn't the first time a girl had run away, but Ariel's situation was especially tricky. "Ms. Sherman, when did you last see Ariel, and did she know about the other girl?"

"At dinner, she went to her room after. I'm not sure if she knew, but it was all over the Internet, so it's likely. Damn it."

"We will find her. Let's start with the other girls—could Ariel be in one of their rooms?"

"I'll go check, but I doubt it. She didn't make any friends. Frankly, she only ever looked happy when she heard from you or Detective Carpenter."

There was no time to even start to process how Ellie felt about this. "Yes, please go check. I'll get the word out to my colleagues."

She hastened back down the stairs to inform Valerie about the situation.

"There's a small chance we're lucky, and she's just hiding out in someone else's room."

"But you don't think it's likely. Poor girl."

"I am calling it in."

There was a lot more than sympathy between the lines of Valerie's words. Her case depended greatly on Ariel and her credibility. They needed to find her safe and sound. Everything else was unimaginable.

She was under incredible stress, and to unleash the city's police force searching for her was likely to add to that.

Ellie had just gotten off the phone when Ms. Sherman joined them again, shaking her head sadly. "None of the girls has seen her since dinner," she said.

"I have notified my colleagues. They'll be on the lookout. We're also going to search the area, and every corner of the house. We'll make sure she's safe."

⟡

Jordan caught up with her a few minutes later, joining Ellie on the meticulous search from attic to basement. There was no sign of Ariel. Eventually, they joined the officers outside. The group home was located near a park, with a hiking trail leading up into the woods from there.

"What is on her mind right now?" Ellie asked out loud. "She's been holding it together except for being a bit disorganized, like most teenagers. Then she hears about Joy Anne—that has to trigger something. She knows the structures in the cult inside out."

"I am fairly certain that she just wants some peace and quiet. It's not knowing how she's going to try to achieve that worries me."

Jordan's tone was level, but Ellie couldn't help thinking of something she had shared another time, of having been in such a dark place that peace and quiet had become an urgency.

"We need to find her soon," she said, not because this was news to Jordan, but because it served as reassurance that they would.

They had almost made it to the beginning of the hiking trail.

Rain had made the ground slippery. Up here, there were still some streetlamps, but the light was sparse enough for them to turn on their flashlights. A quick check in with the other search teams revealed no results so far.

There was a pavilion to the left of the hiking trail. Jordan must have had the same thought because she headed straight in that direction rather than following the trail.

Ellie hurried after her.

Underneath the roof, Ariel sat against one of the pillars, shivering, wearing only a hoodie over jeans and a t-shirt. She didn't look up when they got closer.

"Hey. Ariel." Jordan crouched down next to her while Ellie called off the search. "Let's get you home?"

They both flinched at the word, Ellie noticed. Ariel looked up at them, her expression matter-of-fact even though her face was tear-streaked.

"Everybody's already fed up with me. And if I testify, they'll get to me too."

"That's definitely not true. Look." Jordan sat on the ground next to her. "Hearing about Joy Anne must have been terrible for you. I can promise you, no one's getting to you—no reporters, none of the brothers or people who helped them. We don't know yet if any member of your family threatened Joy Anne, but that's why we wanted to take you to a safer place."

"And we'll be there too," Ellie added, hoping she wasn't promising too much. For sure, the FBI would like to be informed of the proceedings. Maybe Bethany would come, even though she had accepted a promotion recently. It could be a challenge to handle both of Jordan's exes at the same time, but for Ariel's sake, she could certainly do it.

For the first time, she saw a bit of a light in the girl's eyes. "Really?"

"Sure. I'll have to clear it with my sergeant, but I'm sure he'll say yes, and so will Jordan's boss. Ms. Esposito will want to talk to you about your testimony some more, but other than that, we can hide out from everyone and everything until the trial. Have pizza...and you don't even have to make your bed."

Ellie stepped closer and sat to Ariel's right, wincing at the contact with the cold damp floor.

Ariel leaned into her with a tired sigh.

"I wish I could just stay with you." Over her head, Ellie exchanged a look with Jordan, not at all surprised to see her tear up. Ellie assumed that she might be wondering the same thing. What if they could make it happen?

Chapter Eleven

There was no opportunity to raise the question until later that night, and even then, Ellie hesitated. Ariel had taken a hot shower at the house, apologized to Ms. Sherman, and then packed for the safehouse. After conversations with their respective superiors, Ellie and Jordan picked up some clothes for themselves as well, and then they drove Ariel. Valerie Esposito followed.

When she and Jordan sat together in the living room after Esposito had left, Ellie wasn't sure how to approach the subject. She didn't want to disappoint Jordan or Ariel, when she had only little knowledge of the proceedings, when she didn't even know how to feel about the idea.

Could they do it—even think about it? Did they have the resources to care for a child that had survived the traumatic death of her mother, and years in an abusive cult? Most importantly, when Ariel said those words, did she mean it, or were they just showing how overwhelmed and confused she was?

"I wish I could have a drink," she said instead of all the things that were reverberating in her mind.

Jordan laughed softly. "Me too, but I guess that has to wait until after the trial." She paused for a moment, then continued, "Have you thought about applying for another job? I hear one of the guys in Vice just asked for a transfer. They have always been short-staffed."

"Yeah. I don't know. Maybe."

"What are you thinking?"

"The same thing you are thinking about?"

Jordan took a deep breath. "Maybe. I'm not sure what we can do about it."

"Yeah. I know we said maybe for a while now, but have you ever thought about adopting?"

"I have," Jordan confessed. "I'm just not sure I have enough to offer...Jack and Pauline had a damn tough job, and they were up to it at every turn. I hope Ariel gets to have a family like that. I care about her, and I know you do, too."

"But?" Ellie prompted.

"I couldn't stand to be the mother who fails," Jordan said, getting to her feet. "I wouldn't want to put that kind of pressure on any child, to right what my birthparents did wrong."

"What if we got it right? What if we don't get any more signs?"

"You are serious about this?"

"I am—" Ellie's answer was interrupted by the ringing of Jordan's cell phone. She put Derek on speaker.

"Hey, Ellie," he said. "There's good news and...some bizarre stuff. Joy Anne was able to make a statement. She blames the police and the D.A.'s office for trying to influence her against her family, and regarding the bizarre..."

"Oh, that wasn't it?" Jordan sighed.

"She calls Ariel the spawn of the devil. No love lost there."

"Nice. You got anything else?"

"Just because she said it, doesn't mean no one told her to say it."

"Yeah, I agree. Keep an eye on her and keep me posted. We'll see you in court."

Even before Jordan suggested one of them could turn in for the night, Ellie knew she wouldn't get a definitive answer from her tonight, but that was okay. They shouldn't make a decision like that on the spur of a moment—but she felt confident about having raised the question. Ariel shouldn't live in uncertainty for years to come—and neither should they.

By the morning, neither of them had gotten a lot of sleep, but they had continued their conversation, starting the day with a lot more certainty and determination. Their professional lives had often put them in contact with people who could help out with the details. Now it was up to them to raise the question with Ariel, once the time was right.

First, she had to get through her testimony.

⟡

"They hate me, don't they?" Ariel asked over breakfast. "No one has even tried to talk to me."

"Many of them grew up with the Prophets, or have been with them for a long time," Jordan told her. She wasn't surprised the girl's mood had swung somewhat when it came to her family members. It would take more time to come to terms with the fact they didn't care for her all that much. It could take decades. "When you are in a bad situation for so long, you can become convinced that it can only get worse."

"My mom wasn't like that, though. She believed that we could make it outside."

"Yes, and I have no doubt you will. Others might change their mind eventually when they realize they are free."

"Are they, really?" Ariel looked doubtful. "Are you sure all of them will be convicted?"

The bust at the Prophets of Better Days compound had been the largest in this context that Jordan had seen in her career. Yes, she wished all of the abusers could go away for a long time.

"Most of them," she said.

Ariel nodded, as if she'd already come to that conclusion by herself. "Do I have to stay at the home until I'm eighteen?"

That question hit too close to home at this time of the morning. A few months ago, she had promised Ellie that they would start thinking about children once her career was taking off. Ellie had been incredibly patient when it came to Jordan's reservations about moving in together, and now, she was thinking about sharing a house, getting married and adopting a teenager? This was going so fast it was making her head spin—but maybe life wouldn't always wait for her to catch up, even if Ellie did.

"Not if you get adopted. Your father waived his parental rights, so there's nothing in the way."

"I guess that's one good thing he did," Ariel said darkly. A pause ensued in which she apparently remembered her words from the day before. "I know you're trying to help me, and I'm really grateful. I'm sorry I ran away, and what I said yesterday—I know you don't really have the time to always have me around. Not that I can't take care of myself, but...You know."

Ellie poured some more tea into Ariel's cup before she got up to get the coffee pot for Jordan and herself.

"The thing is, we'd love to have you around, but it's something you have to decide too. Actually, we are buying a house...and once this is all over, if you want, you could come look at it, see if you like it."

Obviously, a careful approach was out of the window now. Ariel's eyes widened as the implications set in, hope warring with disbelief. Jordan remembered her first day with Jack and Pauline well, fearing every minute that it could be only a dream.

"I'm sure the house is fine," Ariel said. "I like you...and I know the Prophets taught us that homosexuality is a sin and from the devil, but Mom always said that was a load of bull-shi—crap."

"Ariel." Jordan couldn't help it. If they were going to be parents, shouldn't they start right here?

Ellie laughed. "She's totally right. Prejudice does stink."

Ariel looked happy and excited, but while Jordan was still processing the past few seconds, her mood changed abruptly.

"Okay, right, that sounds nice, now let's forget about it. I'm so sorry. It was stupid of me. Why would you even care when my Dad wants nothing to do with me?"

"Because sometimes family has nothing to do with being related by blood," Ellie said. "I have friends who were disowned and kicked out by their parents, and they met kinder and more open-minded people whom they call family. I know they taught you a very different idea of family, but you already know that's not all there is. And when parents fail, it's okay to call them out on it, hold them accountable. If your Dad doesn't care, that says everything about him, and nothing about you."

"There's paperwork involved," Jordan added, determined not to make this about herself. Ariel needed them now. "Background checks, CPS will visit, and they'll make sure the circumstances are right for you. It might take a little while, and we'll probably have to wait until after the trial to get started—but we'll do our best to make it happen as soon as possible. Once we leave the safehouse—if you want, that is."

"Thank you so much! Yes, I want that." The next moment, Ariel wrapped her in a tight hug, and Jordan hugged her close in return, aware of every single emotion she'd still have to work on herself. She caught Ellie's smile. This was the right decision. They'd be all right.

It might not be easy, but when had that ever stopped them?

Ariel needed a safe environment away from the people who had informed her recent years, time to grieve her mother and adjust to the world outside of the compound. They could provide that for her.

If given the chance. But with their record, who would deny it to them?

They stayed up long past what should have been each of their bedtimes, given the fact that Ariel might have to testify the next day, and both of them would have to as well. The story unfolding had taken precedence over everything else.

Valerie was wrong. This had nothing to do with guilt over her own shortcomings. It was a chance to pay it forward that she wouldn't let pass her by.

Jordan and Ellie kept in touch with Derek who sounded angry when he related that two other women had retracted their statements. They didn't confirm what Joy Anne had said, either, but they didn't want to go on the record against the Prophets.

They did the best they could to distract Ariel from her upcoming gigantic task, with movies and a couple of card games they taught her. There hadn't been much play or connection to pop culture on the inside. It was harrowing to think that within a short time, Ariel might have been "married" and the mother of another child trapped in hell.

Ariel went along with all their efforts. Her presence brought up a lot of memories for Jordan, which, put into context, reminded her over and over again how lucky she'd been. She wanted to be the person who sent this young girl on her own lucky path. Failure was not an option.

They watched an episode of a sitcom after dinner, and then, given the process looming, made it an early night.

"Did we make the right decision?" Ellie asked, her words resonating in the dark, coming out of the blue. Jordan had thought she was asleep.

"Yes, I believe so."

"This is a big deal. We're in all the way, and...I'm fine with that. It's maybe not how we planned to have a child, but if that's the way, I'm good. I just want to make sure it's the same for you."

"Why wouldn't it be?"

Ellie turned to her, snuggling close. "It's a lot happening in a short amount of time. If this is going too fast for you, and I'd understand, I need to know now."

"What do you mean?" Jordan didn't like where this conversation was going. There was no room for doubts or a do-over—not that she needed it. Not anymore. She hoped Ellie knew that.

"The house, and now the new plan...You'll be stuck with me and a teenager for the immediate future. We haven't lived by ourselves much. I just want you to be sure you're okay with all that, because it wouldn't be fair to Ariel if we found out after the fact."

"What do you think?" Jordan couldn't help it, the edge that had crept into her tone. She sat up and reached out to turn on the lamp.

"This is the right thing," she said, keeping her voice deliberately soft. "Ellie. I love you, more than I could ever put into words. This girl has been through hell, and we have something to offer to her. I might not have been raised in a patriarchal cult, but I know what it's like to be offered a way out of something bad. I want to do my best to give her that, and I know that together we can. So, if you're in it, that's good, because I am too."

"I love you too," Ellie whispered. "I wanted to make sure I didn't push you into any of this."

"This is exactly what I want."

It was good to be certain. They needed every bit of certainty going to trial.

The next morning, while Ariel was in the bathroom and Ellie prepared breakfast, Jordan called her parents. Pauline picked up.

"I need to tell you something," Jordan said without pre-amble. "You can tell Jack, but aside from that, neither of you can talk to anyone about it yet. Ellie and I are going to—try anyway—to adopt a child."

There was stunned silence on the other end, before Pauline said, "Jordan, that is amazing, but how...When did you make that decision? I thought you might be...You have to tell me everything. That means you asked Ellie to marry you!"

"No, I didn't ask Ellie yet," Jordan hastened to curb her enthusiasm. Before she could remind Pauline not to talk about this subject to anyone either, Ellie came into the bedroom.

"Ask me what?"

"Pauline wanted to know if we're coming to dinner on the weekend, to tell her everything. She's looking forward to meet-ing Ariel."

"I definitely am," Pauline said, and Jordan congratulated herself on thinking quickly. She had a brief, spare thought for a dying Jonathan Darby—*see how everything in my life is falling into place? You have no more power over any of it.*

"I just wanted to let you know. We'll see you on the weekend, and then we'll talk about everything, I promise. Bye." She ended the call, not wanting to get into the subject too deeply with Ellie at this moment.

The bathroom door opened, and Ariel emerged. Her looking apprehensive came as no surprise, but she was determined. They all were.

"Let's have breakfast," Jordan said. "We don't know how long this day is going to be."

Chapter Twelve

A.D.A. Valerie Esposito was laying out her case, reminding everyone in the courtroom that besides Joseph's murders, and the illegal gun sales, there had been a number of other crimes committed on the compound.

"The man who murdered Ariel's mother is facing a life-long prison sentence," she said as she turned to the jury. "This matters. The testimony you'll hear from Ariel Deane and the other women is about the bigger picture of what happened behind closed doors in the Deane compounds. Not all of the men on trial might have been complicit in the murders, or covered them up, but there's one thing they are all guilty of, without exception.

Every girl who grew up in that place, every woman trapped in there knew that complete obedience and submission was expected of them, and that there would be consequences for any attempt at breaking those rules. Children witnessed many instances of abuse on a daily basis, including a mockery of marriage in which the Deane men involved underage girls. The many children rescued here, in Iowa and Arizona, have a chance now, as long as they can live the rest of their lives far away from the influence of those men. I trust that after hearing a first-hand account of those stories, you will make the right decision. There was some angry grumbling from the defendants' side of the room. Valerie, unfazed, continued to explain how she was going to call Agent Strickland, who had successfully infiltrated the cult, as well as other law enforcement officers who had been confronted with the horrors going on at Prophets'.

Joy Anne Deane, still in a wheelchair, was present as well. Ellie wondered if she was going to testify today. Every testimony of a cult member would add pressure on Ariel and the few women who had been able to tear themselves away.

There was no doubt that the brothers who had originally founded the group, had known about the crimes of one of their members, and covered them up for years. Ariel's testimony mattered for different reasons—it was going to show a pattern of domestic and child abuse, of fake marriages with underage girls and insufficient paperwork regarding the many children in the compound. In other words, one big mess. She and other eyewitnesses were instrumental in making the cases against the men who had benefited from these patterns for a long time.

Dr. Bethany Roberts was in town as well. Ellie had briefly seen her when Valerie was preparing them for their testimony.

It was pretty cut and dried: Joseph had played his family, and tried to play the authorities as well, in an attempt to hide his crimes, all the while building a graveyard in the compound.

Remembering, Ellie had to breathe through the rush of anger. Days like these, everything they did seemed like a drop in the ocean, nothing more. For every Joseph they arrested, there seemed to be a dozen potential more, with the same smug attitude and antiquated ideas about gender. Not all of them became violent...but nothing much changed over time.

❦

Ellie was called not long after Strickland, which wasn't surprising given that she had closely worked with the task force. Valerie asked her to describe the final day of the cult, obviously to show to the jury that everything had been done by the book.

There was no love lost between Valerie, and Bethany who had involved Ellie in the final part of this operation in the first place, but they took care to keep it clear and professional. Ellie wanted to do her part as well.

"I made contact with Agent Strickland, and we were allowed to go to a room. Joseph was supposed to give the FBI a signal. He didn't."

"What happened next?"

"Backup was coming in," she said. "One of the men who had been guarding the door, yelled 'traitor' at Joseph and shot him. We exchanged gunfire, and then my colleagues came in. That is all. We only later found out about the other women Joseph had killed."

The attorney made a half-hearted attempt at an objection, but Ellie was excused. That had almost been too easy. Then again, she wasn't the star of the trial.

She went to find Ariel who was waiting for her turn in an office, accompanied by Ms. Sherman, the door guarded by Libby. Ellie greeted her and went inside.

"Hey. How are we doing in here?"

Ariel hugged her, hard.

"It will be okay, sweetie. I promise." She was aware of Ms. Sherman's surprised gaze, realizing that she and Jordan had a lot to explain to the woman. It might look irrational to an outsider, but for her, Jordan and Ariel, the case that had brought them together was the missing piece. She was certain of it. Life had handed Ariel the worst, taking her mother and leaving her knowing that her father didn't care about her. They could alter the narrative. They would.

"Ariel, do you think I could talk to Ms. Sherman for a moment? We'll be right outside the door."

"Yes, sure. It's not time yet, is it?"

"No. They'll hear more of the officers who were at the compound that day, and then some of the other women. I'll see you in a minute."

"I don't know what you did at that safe house, but it had some effect," Sherman said, "Ariel seems...different. Of course she's still grieving, but for the first time since I met her, she appears less nervous about the testimony. It's a lot for someone this young."

"I'm glad to hear that. Ms. Sherman, we were hoping to get some advice from you. Right now, there's a lot of media attention on this case, so we have to be careful, but...Detective Carpenter and I have made a decision. We'll start the paperwork to adopt Ariel as soon as possible."

The audible gasp hadn't come from Mary Sherman, but Libby, who quickly schooled her features into a neutral expression.

"You talked about that yesterday?" Sherman asked.

"I know what you're going to say, but we did think this through. We just bought a house. Two incomes. We can offer a safe environment to Ariel, and I think the sooner she has certainty as to where she's going to live, the better. As you know, her mother is dead, and her father waived his parental rights. No relatives have come forward. We spoke to Ariel as well. We were hoping you could get us started once Ariel has testified."

"You can come to my office when you're ready. Then we can have that conversation."

"Thank you so much."

Jordan's testimony later that week was fairly uneventful as well—no attorney could argue much with the bodies found in the compound. Ariel was called that afternoon, and she stepped into the witness stand looking pale, but determined as she faced the hostile stares of the men and women sitting with the defendants.

"Ariel, first of all I want to say I'm so sorry for your loss," Valerie began.

"Thanks," Ariel whispered.

"I know this is hard for you, but I think it's important that the jury hears about your and your mother's story. Could you please tell me about Deborah's plans, and when she shared them with you?"

"She wanted to get us out."

Ariel's voice was barely audible, and the judge asked her to speak louder. The girl cleared her throat. "She wanted us to leave, on the night the FBI was supposed to raid the place. She told me only a few days before, but I know she had spoken to Lilly, and they had come up with the plan together."

"By Lilly you mean Lilah Strickland, the agent who was undercover at the house." Strickland, who had given her testimony earlier, had used that name with the cult.

Ariel nodded. "Yes. She wanted to make sure we were safe by the time they came in, but..." She swallowed hard. "Mom never came back."

Ellie felt the tears stinging behind her eyes. This was only the beginning, and if Ariel was supposed to make it through, she and Jordan had to keep it together for her. She cast a quick look at Jordan sitting next to her, her hands held together tightly in her lap.

"Again, I'm sorry. Did your mother tell you why you were going to leave? And why it had to be done in secret?"

"I think she wasn't very happy. She said she had been dreaming about it, but now that Lilah was going to help us, it could be real, that they couldn't come after us."

"Why would they come after you?"

The defendants' attorney jumped to his feet. "Objection. Speculation."

"I'll rephrase," Valerie said coolly. "Did Deborah mention anything specific she wasn't happy about?"

"Yes. A girl that lived with us just got married. She was fifteen, and...it would have been me, next."

Ellie could see the jaw-dropping effect the revelation had on the jury.

"Objection—"

"I heard her talk about it with Dad!" Ariel defended herself. "He said it was time I did my contribution, and that I was old enough. I didn't want to get married. The guy was, like, thirty! And after that, it would all be over, taking care of the babies would be all I'd do."

It wasn't the first time Ellie heard about the practices of the Prophets, but the reality of it never failed to put her in a state of rage.

"I think we can all agree that this would be a good reason for Deborah to part with the family. Your dad made those decisions all by himself?"

"He made all decisions by himself, except when the brothers told him otherwise. I know Mom was only trying to protect me, but she should have left a long time ago. He beat her—because they said that was okay, to discipline the wife when she talks back at you."

"Did he ever hit you?"

There was a pregnant pause. The air was thrumming with emotion, mostly anger, from those in the room who found it unbearable to listen to this account, and from those who were indignant about their secrets being revealed.

Ellie could barely breathe.

"Not that often," Ariel said. "He knew Mom would go crazy on him, and she was around me most of the time." She shrugged. "It happened. You know...They make you think that being born a girl is like a flaw somehow, that you have to work on your whole life. Mom often told me that they were wrong, that I shouldn't think that way, but...it was hard sometimes."

"Well, your mom was right, and we can best honor her memory by acknowledging that."

"That's all sad, but what does it have to do with anything?" the attorney asked.

"Counselor, do you have an objection?" the judge queried, and the attorney sat back down, shaking his head with a sullen expression.

"Good," Valerie said. "This is not going to be easy to hear, and it's not easy for Ariel to do this, but to put all of this into context for you, we'll go through several specific instances that she witnessed in only the past eighteen months. Like we've heard from the other women, the Deanes' lifestyle wasn't just theory, and they enforced it every single day."

"Objection. She's testifying."

"Sustained."

"Sorry, Your Honor." Valerie went back to asking Ariel questions about her day-to-day life with the Prophets.

Ellie laid her hand over Jordan's. They were surrounded by colleagues, not that she cared who saw it at this moment. This couldn't be over soon enough.

⁂

Ariel was holding up, until the defense called Joy Anne Deane who seemed hell-bent on dismantling everything the girl had said. The jury had hung on to every of Ariel's word earlier, but they were just as drawn to the soft-spoken woman in the wheel-chair, Jordan noticed with trepidation. Joy Anne was dressed in a skirt and a blouse, her long hair coming down to the middle of her back. It wasn't quite the look the women living with the Prophets had been forced to adopt, but there was no doubt they went for an appearance that was soft and harmless. The bruises still visible in her face only added to the image.

"I don't mean any harm to Ariel. I know she's been through a lot. But someone needs to tell the truth. I understand that my sisters are prepared to do the same, even though they've been harassed by this department as much as I have."

"Could you explain what you mean by that?" the attorney asked, now a smug expression on his face. Valerie's lips were set in a thin line.

"They put words in my mouth from the beginning," Joy Anne claimed. "It was hell for me and my family. We were all afraid they were going to take our children away from us, based on those accusations."

"Well," he said, "the police made some gruesome discoveries on your grounds. Isn't it understandable that they were worried about the children?"

"But no one knew anything about it except Daniel, and Joseph, of course. We don't claim that no one is ever...tempted by evil. Everyone was shocked, and the police department used that in their agenda against us."

"Objection!" Valerie was on her feet. "There is no proof of any of those accusations, none. We've heard already that the agents and officers working with them were acting well within their competence. They were doing their jobs."

"Let's see. Ariel earlier talked about child marriages on your premises, and polygamy. You have been part of the family for longer than her. Can you tell us about your experiences?"

Joy Anne shook her head, laughing bitterly.

"We might be old-fashioned. People laugh about that these days. That is why we keep to ourselves. In all my time, I haven't witnessed any marriage with multiple girls, and not one with an underage child. We keep a traditional lifestyle—we're not abusers."

"Liar!" A woman's voice was heard, and the judge banged his gavel.

Jordan couldn't see where the interruption had come from. Joy Anne's face reddened. She straightened in her wheelchair.

"Ask yourself who's the liar," she hissed, in a heartbeat shedding the pretense of sympathy and kindness. "They were going to take away everything from us. Deborah could have taken her daughter and left, and the same went for Jennifer, but they didn't. There was no need to drag all our names through the mud. They lie, and they don't care whose lives they are destroying. It's because of them that I saw no hope! It's their fault!"

Ariel started crying.

Jordan exchanged a look with Ellie, and they took the girl outside. After Joy Anne's testimony, the court would be adjourned until the next day. It had been too long already. There was no saying how much damage she would do, and if her words could intimidate the other women.

"I knew she was going to say these things, but it's..." Ariel didn't finish her sentence. They had found a bench in a quiet corner in the hallway, where Jordan held her close.

"I know. I'm sorry you had to go through all this."

"Hey girls, I wanted to say hi...oops, sorry. I didn't mean to interrupt."

Jordan suppressed a sigh at the sound of Bethany's voice.

"That's okay," she said. "We were just trying to get away from the malice."

"I don't blame you. You have a good evening. Ellie." She surveyed the scene. If she was surprised, she was hiding it well. "By the way, I'll be in town for a couple more days, so if you still hang out at the *Night Shift*, maybe we can all have a drink?"

Much to Bethany's credit, the offer was meant for the two of them.

"Maybe, but not tonight. We'll see you tomorrow," Jordan said.

Ariel pulled back and wiped her face. "I think I can go back to the house now that it's clear no one pushed Joy Anne...You guys can go out. I don't want to keep you from anything."

"You're not," Ellie said firmly. "It's true that the safehouse is probably no longer necessary, but we'll come with you. Tomorrow, we'll talk about the next steps with Ms. Sherman. We'll get this done as quickly as possible."

Ariel gave her a tired smile.

"Okay then. I'd still like to be alone for a bit, later, if that's okay. You think they're going to call me again?"

"Of course, and no. We can think about the future now. Let's get you home."

<hr>

Jordan wasn't surprised to hear the warnings from Ms. Sherman. She could tell that the woman had mixed feelings about the proposal, and she didn't blame her. If this worked out for Ariel, the sooner she got into a family, the better. Jordan and Ellie were determined to do whatever they could to make this happen, but there was no doubt Mary Sherman had seen a lot of stories that didn't work out.

Ariel was left with a father who didn't give a damn about his daughter.

This shouldn't take too long, should it?

Sitting at her desk the next day, Jordan allowed herself a moment to fantasize about the future. They had mailed Andrea Cox the signed papers. Everything was in order. The house inspection would come next, giving them an idea about what kind of work needed to be done right away, if any. By the time Ariel could move in with them, her room would be ready.

She wondered if Jack and Pauline had been this guiltily excited once the framework was done and the child from the broken home arrived at their doorstep.

Not the same. Not exactly.

There was no denying, though, that she was excited. And feeling slightly guilty about it—but they would always be aware of the fact that Ariel had a mother who had been ripped away from her by a vicious crime.

"Detective Carpenter, do you have a moment, or are you just busy staring into nothing?"

She sat up straighter, knowing right away that Valerie's question couldn't mean anything good. After they'd broken up, Valerie had refused to call her by her first name for weeks.

"How can I help you?"

"That's a good question. A very good question indeed. Let's go do this in private."

"Sure."

Aware of Derek's questioning look, she shrugged in his direction and followed Valerie to the break room.

"What the hell are you doing?" Valerie asked, enraged. Jordan wasn't sure what she'd done to deserve her wrath.

"Let me rephrase that. Why on earth is Phelps calling you back to the stand?"

"He is?" Jordan frowned. That wasn't good. "Why?"

"I asked you that already. I do have a theory though. Maybe it has something to do with you and your girlfriend getting cozy with the main witness in this case."

"What? He can't question any of that! Both Ellie and I were with other cops the whole time, who can confirm anything we've said. The woman from CPS was on the other side of the window with an agent!"

"I don't think your testimony was the problem. Ariel's is. After Joy Anne did her little spiel, some of the women want to recant. Some say they can't remember, and that it's possible they were coached by the police. I've had one hell of a morning, only to find out that you want to play parent to that girl of all people? Do you really hate me that much?"

"Whoa, slow down, first of all, I don't hate you. Play parent? That's low. We talked this through at the safehouse, and we believe it's the best solution."

Valerie scoffed. "For whom? If Phelps makes that jury think you influenced her, and some of the women, like Joy Anne said, our case starts falling apart. Daniel and Joseph, sure, they won't get away, not even Joy Anne denied that. The others..."

"No. No, that can't be happening. Not just because of my testimony."

"Our office will do its best to keep it from happening. Stay away from the Deane girl for a bit. It's admirable that you want to make sure she's okay, but we can't have anyone think you or any cop in this building coached her, just because you don't like the traditional way of life."

Jordan sat on the bench, silent for a moment. Valerie apparently didn't know the whole story. The papers they'd file would be a matter of public record. Phelps could get that information too.

"Oh no. I sense that there is more. Spill it so I can mentally prepare for kissing those convictions goodbye."

"We want to adopt Ariel," Jordan said. "We spoke to Ms. Sherman who runs the group home today...and we were going to get the paperwork rolling as soon as possible. That has nothing to do with the case or what was going on in Deane's house..."

"Stop," Valerie said. "Just stop."

"No, you listen to me. Is this all inconvenient, maybe, but we're talking about a child. If someone else had butted out when things might have gotten difficult, I wouldn't be here."

"But this is not about you. You better not screw this up," Valerie warned.

"I don't plan to."

Chapter Thirteen

The trial and the events surrounding it had held up a mirror to all of them, Ellie thought when some days later, they picked up Ariel to show her the house, the new home for all of them. The pieces were falling into place—she'd keep looking for an opening as a detective, and meanwhile she would have to live with the fact that her parents weren't here anymore to see her successes, no matter how proud they'd be of her.

Jordan had hinted at some tense conversations with A.D.A. Esposito, and she would have to testify once more, but all things considered, life was on track for all of them.

She could put her own grief behind her, now that Ariel needed her, the girl's grief so much more raw than Ellie's.

After visiting their future home, they would have dinner at Jack and Pauline's and drive Ariel back to the group home after. Once they were in touch with a social worker and had a visit, they might be able to have her over for a weekend soon.

"There's a high school just a few blocks away," Jordan said as they exited the car. "You could probably go there."

"Yeah. I guess they're going to look at my test scores. Mom always made sure they were okay." Ariel had been home-schooled as all the children in the compound. Deborah had worked hard to build a future for her daughter away from the Prophets.

High school would be a drastically different context.

"I know there are a lot of changes coming for you, but we'll take it step by step, okay?"

Ariel nodded. "I'm not scared," she said matter-of-factly. Ellie acknowledged that is was probably true, at least for the moment. After what she'd been through, what was left to be scared of?

"That's okay. Let's go take a look now. We'll have some painting to do, and we wanted to re-do the kitchen as well, but that's pretty much it."

Ellie unlocked the door and walked inside after Jordan and Ariel, all of a sudden emotional with this situation laden with meaning. After the death of her parents, she'd moved into a tiny apartment, not making much of an attempt at turning it into a home. Things changed somewhat after she'd entered the academy, making new friends, eventually meeting Rhonda. The years they'd lived together had come with some good, and not so good moments—it had always been a transitory place. Then Jordan came into the picture. Ellie had lived with her for a short while after her abduction, then moved in with Kate, waiting once more.

The waiting was over. This was where they'd build their life together, with an unexpected yet welcome addition.

"We thought this could be your room," Jordan said as she opened the door and let Ariel in. It was one of three bedrooms upstairs, including the master. Between their bedroom and what was supposed to be Ariel's, there was an office.

Ariel stepped inside, her expression hard to read.

"It's...big," she said. "Are you sure?"

The windows on this side of the house were large, letting in lots of light. Initially, they had imagined this to be a guest room, but the office could always double as such. Ariel's question, however, seemed to signify a lot more than the size of the room.

"Yes, we are," Ellie said, laying an arm around the girl's shoulders. "About everything. It might not go as fast as we hope it could, but eventually, we'll all be in this house, and of course, there will be furniture. I know it's hard to imagine right now."

"It's great." Ariel gave her a brief smile before she stepped to the window. "Mom wished so hard for us to have a place of our own. I hate that she'll never have that."

"She would want you to have it. I'm sure."

"Please don't think I'm ungrateful. I'm so glad I won't have to live with Dad, ever."

Ellie caught Jordan's troubled gaze at the admission. "We understand."

Much more than Ariel was aware of at this moment.

⁂

Jordan began the day with a headache following vague nightmares, the last of what she needed before testifying once more. On the bright side, Ariel had seemed to enjoy dinner with Jack and Pauline, and Ms. Sherman informed them that she did better with the routines at the house. Ellie was already gone when she drove to the courthouse, hoping that both the testimony and the persisting headache would be a thing of the past soon.

Jordan had a fleeting thought wondering about Darby's condition, then decided she had too much on her plate already. The content of the letter was nothing but his usual bluster—he had to try.

Fortunately, she was called less than half an hour after she arrived. Valerie looked serious. Jordan hoped to convey the confidence that nothing would change. The main objective was to keep the women and children from being exposed to further abuse, and the jury would agree.

Phelps greeted her with the familiar smug smile. She had options, a real life. In order to help these women and children have the same, she could bear with him a little while longer. It wasn't like anyone tied her down to be here. Jordan reached for the glass of water in front of her, wishing Ellie was here. Maybe she was coming down with something. A half day would be nice, but they were planning to save up vacation days so they would be able to make the move and Ariel's transition as easy as possible.

"Detective Carpenter, thank you so much for making time."

It's not like I had a choice. Jordan didn't say it out loud, just gave him a nod in acknowledgement.

"We have heard your testimony, of course, and we have heard Mrs. Joy Anne Deane testify how she felt pushed into a certain direction by the detectives conducting the interviews at the time."

"I'm sure you don't want me to say anything that could be interpreted as hearsay, though I can't imagine anyone I work with jeopardizing such an important investigation."

"You're right, I'm not asking for your interpretation. I'm only interested in the work you did in the course of this investigation. You met the main witness, Ariel Deane, early on."

"I told you, we interviewed her right before she was placed in the group home—temporarily."

"You felt for her, I assume."

Jordan had an idea where he was going with this, and she was determined not to let him get to her. "I feel for all of them. We have heard what was going on in those houses."

"Yeah...We have mostly heard from Ariel. According to Mrs. Joy Anne Deane, much of what we heard was a mix of exaggeration and fantasy, and some of the other women have expressed doubts about her story—"

"Objection!" Valerie snapped. "There is no reason for calling the witness's trustworthiness into question. It makes a lot more sense for your witness, Mrs. Joy Anne Deane, to show loyalty to the members of the sect. Ariel has many more options open to her now."

"Overruled, but please, get to an actual question, Counselor."

"I'm sorry, Your Honor. Here's my question, Detective. Did you, at any time, feel you had to make sure Ariel would say the right words so all these families that you suspected to be abusive, would be broken up? That fathers and husbands would go to prison?"

"I didn't have to put words in her mouth. Besides, the bodies buried in the backyard, and the pretend marriages with minors pretty much spoke for themselves."

"Yes, but we're not talking about those bodies right now. There were many men, women and children who didn't know about them. Does the idea of a traditional lifestyle with clearly defined roles, make you uncomfortable?"

Jordan felt the heat rising up her back. If the jury came to doubt the guilt of the men who had committed years of domestic abuse, but didn't know about the murders, Ariel's father might go free. He might change his mind. That couldn't happen. She cast a look past Phelps at the family members, journalists and otherwise interested, flinching at the sight of the young man, third row, who was looking straight at her, smiling.

Marcus Holmes.

How was that possible? He had confessed the murder of Colin Buck. He made a "thumbs up" gesture, leaving no doubt that he had sought her out. Or had he?

"Detective Carpenter?"

"It's my job to investigate allegations of abuse and arrest criminals, regardless of whose lifestyle I'm more or less comfortable with. Please, Mr. Phelps, don't put words in my mouth."

She caught another glance at Holmes.

"You and your partner are trying to adopt Ariel Deane, regardless of the fact that she does have a living biological parent?"

"I believe that's not the subject of this trial, but I'm sure you're aware that biological parent, Nathan Deane, has no interest in his daughter."

"Please, yes or no, will you try to gain custody of Ariel Deane?"

"This has nothing to do with—"

"Detective, please answer the question," the judge intervened.

"Yes."

"Thank you," Phelps said triumphantly. "That's all I wanted to know."

Valerie was already standing, and Jordan resigned to the fact that she wasn't going to leave the stand anytime soon.

Marcus Holmes was gone.

Fortunately, she found a bottle of Advil in one of her desk drawers.

"Bad day?" Derek asked sympathetically, as he stopped by her desk. He had also brought coffee and donuts. For a moment, Jordan forgot about all pains, physical and otherwise, of the day.

"Thank you so much. I could kiss you." She took the two pills with coffee and leaned back in her chair, inhaling the scent of the beverage.

"Don't make this awkward, please."

"Sorry about that. To be honest, I had more than my dose of awkward already. Valerie is not happy with me, the brothers' sleazy lawyer enjoyed the show, and what the hell is Holmes doing out of prison?"

"Whoa." Derek sat in his chair. "I didn't know about Holmes. I heard some other things though...You and Ellie are really going to adopt the girl?"

"Yeah, I don't think there's a person in town who doesn't know it yet. Before you start, yes, I have looked at all my issues, and I still want to do it. She deserves a chance."

"I'm not arguing," he said, holding up his hands. "I think it's great that you're doing it. If anyone can relate to what she's going through, it's you."

"Except that my parents are very much alive." Jordan sighed. "I want to do what's best for her. We might have been quick to decide, but Ellie and I have talked about it. We do have the means. We care about her." Finally, the headache was starting to recede. "I'm not sure what to make of Holmes coming to the trial though. Why would he even be interested in that, other than sending me some sort of message?"

"We can find out with a call," Derek said, already picking up his phone. It rang before he could make the call.

"This is Detective Henderson."

Jordan went back to the report she'd opened, still infinitely grateful for the supply of sugar and caffeine. She'd work some overtime to catch up, but hopefully Ellie was free later for a real dinner. When she glanced at Derek again, she knew instantly that something was wrong, the certainty turning her stomach even before he ended the conversation. She and Ellie had done well for some time, leaving the more traumatic events further in the past, but the damn letter had stirred up something. Or the bodies buried on the Prophets' compound had.

"We'll be right there," Derek said and hung up. "There was a 911 call at Lori Gleason's house."

He didn't need to elaborate. Jordan was on her feet and in her coat a moment later.

"There are unis on the scene," he explained as they hurried to his car. "Apparently, there's an intruder. She locked herself in her bedroom."

"The member of a serial killer fan club gets a murder charge dropped, and there's an intruder at Gleason's house? That's no coincidence. Darby can't die soon enough."

"I can understand why you feel that way, but this might be a coincidence," he reminded her.

"That's a nice way of saying he's been trying to manipulate me the whole time, and I'm falling for it? I don't care. I'd rather be wrong in the end than miss something here."

Lori Gleason was the first of Darby's victims who had been found alive. She and Judy Lawrence had later founded an advocacy group. Each of them had gone on with their lives best they could. The last time Jordan had seen them she had given each of them her personal number but warned them to always call 911 first.

When Jordan had first met Lori, she'd been separated from her husband. She still lived in the same house. There were two squad cars parked in front, and the front door stood open. Officer Libby Marshall greeted them.

"What's the situation?" she asked.

"The intruder is gone. Ellie and Casey are with Ms. Gleason now, see if he took anything."

"He. Did she get a glimpse of him?"

"Briefly, from upstairs. Black clothes, mask. Nothing special. She locked herself in the bedroom and hid under her bed with the cell phone."

The image sent a shiver down her spine. If he'd had enough time, the bedroom would have probably been the first place he looked. But perhaps he didn't mean to take her.

Jordan was certain that whoever had broken into Gleason's home knew exactly who he was targeting—but Colin Buck was dead, and Marcus Holmes wouldn't be stupid enough to take the risk after he'd just avoided prison?

When they entered the house, Lori Gleason was standing in the foyer with Ellie and Officer Casey Lyons, her arms wrapped around herself as if she were freezing. When she saw Jordan, she left the other two women standing and came to her, for a moment seeming unsure what to do. Then she wrapped Jordan into an unexpected, tight embrace.

"Thank you so much for coming," she said.

"No problem."

"It's never over, is it?"

Jordan didn't want to answer this question at the moment.

"You'll be fine. I promise. Did he take anything?"

Lori stepped back, shaking her head. "No. I have no idea what he wanted from me, but I'm glad the police came before I could find out. I was glad to hear Darby is dying. I never thought I'd say that about a human being."

To call him a human being was probably generous, but Jordan didn't want to get into specifics with the woman. "I need you to think. Have you noticed anyone around lately that stood out, or has someone been following you?"

"No, not that I'm aware of. I'm sorry."

"That's fine." Jordan walked around the room, into the kitchen/living area. Something was missing, even if it wasn't any physical object. The place looked clean, no clutter. What did the intruder want? Was he aware of Gleason's connection to Darby?

Harm her? Or send a message? She opened cabinets and closed them again.

"Did he come up the stairs?" she asked Lori.

"I don't know...I don't think so."

He stayed downstairs...did what he wanted to do and then left. Maybe it was done long before the police arrived.

"You're looking for something?" Ellie asked behind her.

Jordan stopped in front of the huge fridge. A number of photographs, menus and flyers were stuck to it with magnets, souvenirs from various states. One picture, an old-fashioned photograph taken with an instant camera, was partially hidden underneath a Thai food takeout menu. Jordan reached out with a gloved hand and drew the menu aside. She recoiled at the sight, and she could hear Ellie gasp.

The photograph showed a woman, tied to a chair, in the exact same position they had found Lori Gleason.

Chapter Fourteen

Ellie felt sick to her stomach at the sight of the photo, and she could only imagine what was going on in Jordan's mind. Of course, when the 911 call came in, everyone remembered Lori Gleason's name. Up until now, a coincidence could have been possible—not any longer.

Whoever had come into her house and left the picture, not only wanted her to relive the terror, but they had likely taken another woman. It was starting anew.

"She could still be alive."

"We're going to find out." Jordan was already on her phone. "Let's get this to the lab ASAP. All of it," she added with regard to the various items stuck to the fridge.

Ellie looked behind where Casey was trying to console Lori Gleason.

"Are you okay?" she asked.

"I'm fine." Jordan gave her a shrug. "I want you and Casey to start looking around at places that still sell those cameras, and supplies."

"There might be more than we think. They've made a comeback recently, haven't they?"

"Yeah. But we have to start somewhere."

"Sure. I got you. We'll let you know if we find anything," Ellie promised.

"Thanks."

Ellie and Casey left while Jordan stayed behind to help Lori Gleason find a place to stay for a couple of days. Libby went to take the items from the fridge to the lab.

"This is bad news," Casey stated the obvious when they were outside.

"Yeah." They couldn't let anything derail them now. Their plans for the future were too important. Out of the blue, the thought crossed Ellie's mind that it might help their adoption prospects if they were married. She couldn't think about it now. There was either a new killer on the loose, or someone who aspired to be.

❦

"Do you think he's going to come back?" Lori asked when they waited outside for her friend to pick her up.

"I don't know," Jordan said honestly. "I don't think so, but we want to make sure you're safe."

"And Judy?"

"We'll go see her, too." The intruder had obviously known that Lori Gleason was one of the women who had made it out of Darby's torture chamber. It wasn't a big reach to assume he might be aware of the other survivors.

"Please tell her I'll call her as soon as this is sorted out," Lori said. "Here's Maggie," she said as a car pulled up to the curb. "Thank you."

To Jordan's relief, she didn't try to hug her again.

Fifteen minutes later, they sat in Judy Lawrence's kitchen. The alarm on the woman's face when she realized who their visitors were, was telling.

She, too, had heard about Darby's declining health, but she hadn't observed anything out of the ordinary in the past weeks.

"I work. I cook meals, I clean my apartment. As long as I do these things, I'm all right," she said. "The group I started with Lori was a great help at first, but it became too overwhelming. I don't handle stress very well. I'm not sure I want to know."

"It might be nothing, but we want you to be aware."

"Is Lori okay?"

"She wasn't hurt. It looks like the man who was in her house wanted to scare her, but she's staying with a friend for now. I'd prefer if you do the same."

"For how long?" She looked away, well aware that Jordan couldn't give her a definitive answer to that question.

"A few days, just to make sure we're on the right track. We will find him."

"I believe you. I guess I'll go pack a bag. I can invite myself to my sister's house for a bit."

"What about you? Shouldn't you stay with a friend tonight?" Derek asked when they were driving back to the station.

"Please. We're talking about someone who admires a serial killer. I survived the real thing, remember? Besides, good luck to him figuring out where I stay any given night, these days."

Derek wasn't entirely happy with that answer, but he let it go. "So, you're closer to getting into your new house?"

"Definitely. Which is good, because when we get the visit from social services, we want to make sure there's furniture in Ariel's room. If you have time this weekend, you're more than welcome to help us paint."

"Sure. You showed it to Kate yet?"

"No, I haven't seen her. I don't think Ellie has. She called you?"

"No."

"All right. Let's see what they have on the stores and call it a day."

By the time they left the department that night, it was too late to see Ariel or to even try a home cooked meal. A table at the *Night Shift* and a plate of nachos would do, though Jordan didn't have much of an appetite. The feel of Lori's embrace lingered. It was a confrontation with emotions she didn't have any use for at the moment.

A handful of stores that did photo services and sold supplies had been closed by the time Ellie and Casey arrived.

Jordan's patience had been wearing thin in the course of the day, and she reached her limit when she saw Marcus Holmes sitting at the counter, nursing a beer and waving to her when their eyes met.

"That's enough."

"Not a good idea. Come on. Let it go," Derek warned.

"The hell I will. I want to know what he's up to."

"Jordan. Let's sit for a moment."

She ignored Ellie as well and walked over to Holmes whose smile broadened when she sat on a barstool next to him.

"Detective Carpenter, what a coincidence. You like to come here after work? I noticed a lot of cops."

"Cut the bullshit. Why are you here?"

"Why not? I'm a free man, thanks to a system that works."

"Really. You confessed to a murder."

He shrugged, taking a sip of his beer. "My lawyer helped me a great deal. I realized I didn't remember all the events correctly. I found Colin...and I just blanked out for a while. A good friend of mine died, so obviously, I was under lots of stress. Maybe I just wanted to get out of there, so I said I did it, or maybe I wasn't even sure that day. My lawyer helped me sort it all out."

"You were friends with Colin Buck?"

"What are you saying, that guys like me can't be friends with nerds? That's such a cliché. I miss him."

Jordan ordered a beer and turned to Holmes again. "With Jeffrey Bishop...his pseudonym was obvious. Why do you call yourself The Knight online?"

"Why? You don't think I have something to offer to women?" he asked with a wink.

"Let me ask you one more time. Why are you here? You noticed that there are lots of cops. Some of us wonder why you'd choose this place. Some, I'm sure, don't like you here."

Holmes laughed. "You're not threatening me, Detective, are you? Because that would be a bad move, and I think you're smarter than that. Don't you want some answers before Darby dies?"

"You have answers? Good. I'm going to need them. There's been an incident that would seem to hint at Darby, but he's wasting away behind bars. You being such a big fan of his, you're the closest person for me to look at."

"Am I now? I'm afraid you might overestimate me. Yes, we pulled that little stunt with Colin, having him talk to Darby and report back to us. It was pretty exciting. Think of it as kids trying out a Ouija board. I mean, a real-life serial killer, who has the chance to hear directly from someone like that?"

"Oh yes. It's a real trip."

"It's like watching the tiger from the other side of the glass, hoping it won't break. I understand it's different for you. You were in there with the beast."

Jordan thought his metaphor was completely off and insulting to a beautiful species.

"Mr. Donovan claims that Colin never talked to Darby. Darby, however, says he did. Who's telling the truth?"

"Hell if I know, but then again, it's not really my problem, is it? Maybe Colin lied to us. Maybe Darby lied. You should ask him...since we can't ask Colin."

Jordan knew she should have left it at that. Something else bothered her. It might have been wiser to let it go, for her sake, but she couldn't afford to overlook anything, not with Darby involved.

"In your fan club, you talk about the women a lot? You get off on that?" She couldn't bring herself to say "victim."

"Please, let's be nice. We were mostly interested in the psychological aspects of what drives someone like him, but yes, we thought of the profile of the victims as well." There it was. "The ones who died, the ones who made it out? You did. You tell me, Detective, was it mere luck or something else?"

"Stay away from Lori Gleason and Judy Lawrence. And me. Otherwise, you might not enjoy your freedom for long."

Jordan picked up her beer and went back to the table. Ellie cast her a worried look.

"Is everything okay?"

"It's fine. Did anyone order something to eat? I'm starving."

⚬

They turned in soon after arriving at Ellie's apartment, anticipating an early workday. Ellie lay awake, aware of Jordan sleeping restlessly next to her. It didn't seem like the night terrors they both had experienced at one time or another, so she decided to let her sleep, still deeply disturbed by yesterday's events. It seemed like the new generation of instant cameras were available everywhere. There was no point in freaking out the city by releasing the picture...but they needed an ID on the woman, potentially reported missing. A woman tied to a chair in a basement like Darby's.

They might not be able to save her.

She finally admitted defeat, dressed and powered up her laptop.

What she found after browsing a few sites, made her groan in frustration. On the website of a local newspaper, there was an article, with the picture of the unknown woman front and center.

By the morning, they were going to be swamped with calls from panicked citizens before the doors of those stores she needed to visit, even opened. Ellie recognized the name on the by-line, the woman who had waited for her outside the department after she'd saved mother and daughter from a burning car.

Who had given this to her?

Ellie flinched when a floor plank creaked. Jordan was standing in the doorway.

"Do I want to know?"

"It will be hard to avoid. The picture will be all over the press by the time we are at work."

Jordan hid a yawn behind her hand. "Maybe it's for the better. Someone's bound to have seen her."

"Someone leaked this to her. This kind of picture is not meant for a front page."

"You're right." Jordan started preparing the coffeemaker before she sat next to Ellie. "But...There is something strange about it. The whole set-up."

"You think Holmes and his friends are behind this?"

"He was trying to make me believe they're not out for murder. Maybe he was telling the truth. I'm not sure yet. Let me have a look."

"You've looked at it from every possible angle. There was nothing to identify the person or the background."

"Yeah. Hm."

"You're not making any sense."

"That's because we're having breakfast at four in the morning." Jordan shuddered. "Well, at the moment that's better than sleeping. I wanted to make sure Lori and Judy were out of harm's way...This might not be what we think it is."

"How?"

"I don't know yet."

"Okay." Ellie got up to take two cups and plates out of the cabinet. "I guess we have to wait until later. Maybe we're lucky and someone remembers the woman. Meanwhile...Have you heard anything from Valerie? Or Phelps?"

"No. I hope that was the end of it, and we'll be able to move forward."

"Yeah. It's funny," Ellie said as she poured coffee for the both of them. "I always thought I'd have kids at some point. I just didn't think they'd come half grown up already."

Jordan pondered her words for a moment. "Kids? Plural?"

Ellie laughed. "It's not something we have to decide right now. I'm happy we're doing this with Ariel, and that she wants to be with us."

"Yeah, me too. I get the feeling that whatever else will change, getting up in the middle of the night to talk cases, won't." Jordan seemed to have something else on her mind, but when she didn't continue, Ellie said, "It will be great. I don't expect it will always be easy, but you know that already. It's all going a bit fast, but that's the way it is, and so far, we've been doing okay."

Jordan gave her a grateful smile. "What about you? Do you have any other interviews planned?"

"Not at this moment, no. I know something will come along."

"I have no doubt."

At this point, there was no room for any.

As Ellie had predicted, there were lots of worried calls to the police department, and some harsh criticism for the newspaper. When Jordan walked past the desk where Libby Marshall was diligently fielding calls, the officer gestured for her to stay.

"I think we have something," she said, and Jordan picked up the phone.

"This is Detective Carpenter."

"Yes, my name is Pam. I think I know who the woman in the picture is."

"You know her name? Can you tell me when you last saw her?"

"Um, a minute ago. It's my roommate Tara."

"Pam, where are you?"

"I'm on campus right now. Tara is in the shower."

"Is she all right?" Had Tara made it out of the place where she'd been held, by herself, and told no one?

"Yes, I think so. I...I think she hasn't seen the picture yet."

"Make sure you stay with her in your room. I'll be right there." Jordan hung up. "Great job. Please find Derek and tell him to meet me there," she told Libby, handing her the address Pam had given her, before heading out.

Whatever the verdict, apparently the woman in the picture was alive and physically unharmed. That was a big victory for the day.

Chapter Fifteen

"They gave me a thousand bucks, said it was for a horror movie. All I had to do was sit in the chair, and they put some make-up on me, fake blood. I had no idea they were going to use it that way!"

"Okay. Who are they?"

Tara Rhett was indeed unharmed, and shocked once she discovered that the picture she'd taken had initiated a search for a missing, possibly murdered woman.

"A bunch of guys and a girl making an independent movie. I thought it was a bit creepy, but I've done similar stuff before, and since the girl was with them, it seemed okay. They had it all set up professionally..."

Jordan looked to Derek, and he shrugged, no more inclined to understand why anyone would think this was just fine. If anyone wanted to use Darby's scenes to create a movie, they had pretty questionable tastes in the first place—but as long as no one got hurt, it wasn't up to her to judge.

However, someone had made sure they believed a crime had been committed, and that person had invaded Lori Gleason's house.

"We are extremely glad you didn't get hurt. Can you tell us a little more about them? What they looked like, how you found them?"

"It was online," Tara said, to no one's surprise. "They had an ad on *MadMarket*, saying they were looking for an actress to shoot stills to promote a horror movie, and to use in a trailer. I assumed it was something in the early stages."

"Where did you shoot those scenes?"

"I can show you. It's not far from here."

The day was just getting better.

⸎

None of them was surprised when they arrived at the location to find an empty building. Jordan had expected something like that. She hoped that the crew they'd brought with them would be able to uncover hints as to who was behind the "horror movie."

Tara shrugged. "They even paid for my food on top of the money. Really, I didn't think I was doing anything wrong." Her eyes widened, as if the thought had only now occurred to her. "You guys aren't going to charge me with anything? They lied to me."

"We're aware," Jordan assured her, looking around the vast empty space of the warehouse. Someone had cleaned up.

The ad was long gone from the website where Tara had found it, and getting information on the poster would take time, if they ever succeeded. Jordan was still optimistic. There had to be something. The initiator of this scheme had been cocky enough to walk into Lori's house. He would make a mistake.

She saw one of the CSU techs bag a long dark thread.

"Do you remember anything else?"

Tara was silent for a long time. Jordan had almost given up on getting an answer, when she said, "Actually, yes. They used a really old camera, not one of those you can buy everywhere today. My Grandma had one of them."

"You didn't think that was strange?"

"Actually, no. They told me they were going for the feel of the old-fashioned slasher movies."

It was something that might help them shift the focus. Hopefully, soon, Judy and Lori could go back to their homes and lives, and so could the rest of them. She excused herself when her cell phone rang.

"Kathryn, I'm at work. Is something wrong?" she asked, barely managing to keep the impatience out of her voice. Talking to her birthmother always put her in that state, though she had gotten better lately.

"Oh no, sorry about that. I just wanted to know if you asked Ellie yet?"

"Why?" This time, the irritation came through.

"You're my only child, and exciting things are happening in your life."

No kidding.

"Don't worry about it," Kathryn said. "She'll say yes."

It was questionable whether she could trust in Kathryn's judgment in general, but Jordan had to grudgingly admit she had a point. Ellie would say yes—and Jordan was nervous about asking her.

"I hope so. Look, I have to go."

"That's okay. Let me know if there is any news?"

"I'll call you," Jordan said without committing to anything specifically. There was one way to get over her reservations—make it as soon as possible.

Some of the pieces were coming together.

In the same online marketplace where Tara had found the horror movie ad, Paul Burton, a photographer, advertised vintage cameras and supplies. Ellie called the number, a cell phone, and Burton agreed to meet her at his studio.

He was waiting on the curb when she arrived. "I must admit it was a bit startling to have the police call me—at first I thought it was one of those scam attempts."

"This is real," Ellie assured him. "Could you tell me if you get a lot of traffic from *MadMarket*?"

"Most of it," he said. "But I have to tell you that I meet very few in person. I sell all over the country."

"Then it wouldn't be hard to trace an instant camera or supplies you recently sold to someone local?"

"Funny that you ask about that. A guy came in a while ago, paid cash. Come with me, I can show you what he bought."

"That would be helpful, thank you." Ellie followed him around the corner and down a flight of stairs. He produced the key to a door leading to a basement studio that was filled with cameras, films and other supplies that seemed ancient in the digital age.

"Wow. You have some treasures here."

"I agree, but not everyone values them anymore. Let me check something."

He found an agenda on the cluttered desk. "Yeah, that was last week. I remember it because he blocked the neighbor's car, and I went outside with him when they honked. No one has any patience anymore, right?"

Ellie wasn't feeling extremely patient at the moment. Was this the breakthrough?

"You said you could show me the camera?"

"Oh yes, it was one like this. The same model, actually. Your parents or grandparents might still own one of them."

Ellie didn't correct him. She couldn't let herself get distracted. "Those still work?" She remembered the actress's statement.

"Sure, with the right film."

"Can you describe the customer to me?"

"I'm sorry, I'm no good with people's faces. Young, brown hair, I think...but I can tell you he drove a red Volvo."

"Do you remember anything about the license plate?"

"Something B2...I'm sorry, I didn't get the rest."

"That's okay," Ellie told him though she had secretly hoped for more. She thought of something else and looked for a picture of Holmes on her phone that she showed to the photographer. "It wasn't him?"

Burton shook his head right away. "No. He was about the same age though."

"Okay. Thanks again."

"Glad to help. Have a good day, Officer."

Ellie drove back to the station, where she found Jordan and Derek in the conference room, moments before a meeting with the lieutenant. She passed on what she had found out at Burton's.

"Good job," Derek said just as Lieutenant Carroll walked inside. "You'll check for that Volvo?"

"I'm on it," Ellie promised, hoping that her future boss had overheard the small exchange.

By the end of her workday, she had narrowed the number of owners to less than a dozen, though not yet sufficiently enough to move forward from there.

She was happy to call it a day when Jordan came to her desk and asked if she was ready to go.

"I thought we could check in with Ariel and have dinner after. I made reservations."

"In the middle of the week? What's going on?"

"Nothing. I felt like something other than bar food, and I don't think either one of us is going to cook tonight."

"Cool. We can go home to change after seeing Ariel."

Ellie was almost certain that there was something else on Jordan's mind. Jordan would tell her later, no doubt. Come to think of it, with the decisions made lately, they had something to celebrate.

"This weekend we paint, but after that, maybe she could come spend some more time with us," she suggested.

"Yes, that would be great."

It occurred to her that in spite of the recent tribulations, Jordan appeared happy, not shaken by the curious connection to Darby's case. Soon, he'd be out of their lives for good. Ellie was careful not to wish anyone harm, but it was hard to deny that this man's death would be a relief for many. How anyone could find him an inspiration was beyond her.

She rang the doorbell of the group home twenty minutes later, sharing a look with Jordan that reflected what they both thought and hoped: Soon, they wouldn't have to come back here. Most of the girls rescued from the compounds had family members, often the mothers, to take care of him. Others had already been placed into foster care, or their adoption was in progress. It was a huge effort to clean up the mess the brothers had created. Ellie was proud that they could play a part in that, going beyond what their jobs required.

An employee opened the door to them.

"Thank you for coming," she said. "Mary was trying to reach you, but she will talk to you now."

Her tone alarmed Ellie instantly, and judging from Jordan's expression, she had picked up on it too.

"Is everything all right with Ariel?"

"She's fine. Mary is in her office."

"Thanks."

They walked along the hallway in silence. Jordan knocked on the door, and they entered. Mary Sherman got up from behind her desk to greet them.

"It's good that you're here," she said.

"We wanted to talk to Ariel," Jordan told her. "What's going on?"

"There has been a new development," Mary said, and even before she went on to explain, Ellie felt like someone had knocked the wind out of her. Perhaps, up until that moment, she hadn't truly understood how important it was to her to have Ariel come live with them, to make sure she'd be forever free from the restraints of the life she'd known in the compound.

"What does that mean? We have all our papers in order." Jordan had put on her interrogation tone. Sherman wasn't all too impressed.

"I'm so very sorry. I know you were serious, but there's an aunt of Ariel's who got in touch with us. She hasn't been in the country for some time, but she wants to take care of her."

Silence settled over the room as they were both stunned.

"How is she related to Ariel?" Jordan asked eventually.

"She's her mother's sister."

"Oh, good, then she's probably not into that patriarchal crap." Ellie's throat was tightening with each word, and her attempt at sarcasm failed badly. She didn't even know what to say, or think, other than this was a nightmare. A blood relative. Would she really be better for Ariel? The girl had never mentioned her. "Did you talk to Ariel yet?"

"I did. This is the reason why I'm glad you came. It's hard to tell how she feels."

"If we were to fight this, the blood relative would likely win," Jordan concluded.

"Yes."

"But we could. Besides, why didn't we ever hear about her before? Even if she was out of the country, we tried to find relatives other than the ones in the cult."

"I don't know all the details. She would like to meet you though and thank you for your efforts."

"I'd like to meet her as well, believe me," Jordan said. "Could we have a moment?"

"Of course. I can imagine this comes as a surprise."

"It certainly does."

As soon as Mary Sherman had closed the door behind her, they moved at the same time, embracing each other tightly. Neither of them wanted to be the first to talk, Ellie reflected, because words would easily shatter the fantasy they had built over the past weeks. She felt tears prickle behind her eyes, unwilling to give in to the emotion. But she could no longer stay silent.

"We're going to lose her." Ellie didn't even have the energy to try and make it a question.

"We don't know that yet. We have to meet the woman. If there's any doubt..." Jordan let her words trail off. What she'd said earlier was still true. A court would likely side with biological family. There could be bias against a lesbian couple. Most importantly, did they really want to put Ariel through another trial after what she'd just endured?

"I don't think I feel like going out today."

"I understand, but we have to eat something anyway. I guess we could just cancel and go elsewhere. It doesn't matter." Jordan sounded heartbroken.

"This sucks." It might not be the most mature thing to say, but it worked for Ellie. "Damn it. Why didn't we ever hear about this sister? If she is so qualified to take care of Ariel, why did she never try to help her and Deborah while they were basically locked up at the brothers'?"

"We're going to find out, learn every detail that we can," Jordan said. She was clearly steeling herself. "Ellie...I know we had our hearts set on this happening, but this woman is Ariel's family. If she's serious and not a total screw up, this might be a good thing."

"Are you serious?" Ellie wasn't there yet, not by a long shot, and she assumed Jordan was only putting on a brave face to get them through the next hour or so. "We spent the past few weeks telling Ariel and everybody that family by blood doesn't have to mean anything."

"That is still true, but sometimes it does. Come on. Let's talk to Ariel. We owe her that."

⁂

"I don't understand!" Ariel was in tears. "Mom barely ever mentioned her, so why should I believe her?"

"She seems nice from what Mrs. Sherman told us," Jordan said. The day that had started out so well was slowly turning into a disaster. There had to be some positive outcome in this. Becca Crane wasn't Kathryn, a teenager overwhelmed with her circumstances. She might have her reasons for not contacting Deborah in years, or she had tried and been rejected. Dr. Crane had a daughter of her own. Perhaps she had more to put into her side of the scale. That didn't mean they'd give up easily. But they also had to consider, all of them, that this might not be a fight they could win. It was surreal. There they'd thought they could talk to Ariel about the colors she wanted for her bedroom.

"You're okay with this?" Ariel asked in disbelief.

"No. No, I'm not, we're not, because that is not what we planned. But this is not about me, or Ellie. It's about you, and if it turns out that your mom's sister cares about you, and she's able to raise you, we might have to accept that. You are the most important person in this."

"Am I really? For a moment there I thought now that the case is closed, and you have my testimony, you don't need to make any more promises."

"Ariel, that's not true and you know it."

"If you can't have me, why are you even here?"

"Mary just told us," Jordan explained. "Listen, this is important. When your aunt Becca arrives, and you both are okay with going forward, it's all good. If you ever have doubts or feel unsafe, let one of us know."

Ellie cast her a surprised look, knowing that this promise was potentially hard to keep.

"That's true. You can always call us," she said.

"That sounds like an experiment to me. See how the cult kid adapts to different environments."

"It's not." Ellie looked like she couldn't stand to be in the room much longer. Jordan hated to prolong her pain, but then again, this wasn't about either of them.

"Ariel," Ellie continued. "We could go to court over this, but only if we have good reasons. What you went through on the compound, that counts. But they won't choose us over a family member who is qualified and willing."

"Yeah, I guess. So I wait until Becca comes to pick me up. Thanks for hanging out with me, both of you. And your parents are very nice," she said to Jordan.

"They loved you too. I promise we'll be in touch. We'll meet with your aunt Becca, too, and we'll make sure she's okay."

"All right. I'd rather be alone right now."

"Ariel, it's going to be okay. We won't let you down."

Jordan sat in front of Ariel and took her hands. Ariel made no move to withdraw from the touch.

"I mean it, and Ellie does, too. If anything doesn't feel right, let us know."

Ariel looked up, then past her at Ellie, her sullen expression changing rapidly.

"I'm scared," she whispered.

Jordan watched Ellie wipe her face angrily with a paper tissue. She felt like she had run out of words, to explain, to console either of them. How could they have expected such a bombshell? This was supposed to be a regular visit, to talk, to plan, to be clear that they were going to move forward. And she had planned something else, to take an hour or two out of the day to unwind, have a nice dinner and a glass of wine, and tell Ellie that she wanted to spend the rest of her life with her, make it official.

Now was definitely not a good moment for a marriage proposal.

The change of pace made her antsy, as if they were going to run out of time.

They had other things to worry about. Jordan remembered how hard it had been to trust in any sort of stability after first moving in with Jack and Pauline. She had been afraid that they might send her back, and afraid that they wouldn't. It had taken a long time to understand that she had done nothing wrong.

She hoped they had done enough to reassure Ariel of the same thing.

"I really want to go home," Ellie said. She shook her head. "I don't even know why I just did this when I'm going to cry again. Let's get some takeout quick."

"Sure."

"Ariel is freaking out. I would be too."

"She was okay when we left. Let's see what Becca Crane has to tell us. We'll go from there."

After a quick dinner with the evening news, they decided to call it an early night. Sex had not been on their minds, but when Ellie snuggled into her arms, and Jordan kissed her shoulder softly, she found it hard to stop herself. The warm skin under her lips, Ellie's quiet sigh, ignited a spark that left her both excited and feeling guilty.

They weren't going to forget about the tasks ahead, the lives on the line. Nevertheless, their plans had been derailed today, and their shared intimacy had always helped them move ahead.

Ellie turned to her, and their lips met in a passionate kiss. Her nightgown was riding up, and Jordan took advantage, touching, kissing her way down every square inch of skin revealed. Soon, Ellie wasn't so quiet anymore.

"Shh," Jordan whispered out of habit.

Ellie didn't quite oblige, but she followed Jordan's guidance in every other way.

If only everything else could have been this easy...

*

The next morning, Ellie was still working on finding the owner of a specific dark red Volvo when Kate reached her.

"Hey, how are you doing?" Truth be told, Ellie felt bad about not contacting her. The time seemed to have flown by since Kate had all but run from the city and her job.

"I'm fine, but I guess I should ask you that. I knew about the house, but Libby tells me you and Jordan are going to adopt the girl from the cult? What else don't I know?"

Ellie sighed. "What you don't know is that it's not going to happen. Ariel's aunt turned up from out of nowhere. For some reason, no one knew about her. We'll meet with her...but there's not much of a chance."

"Have you talked to a lawyer?"

"We want to talk to her first. There's no need to expose Ariel to any more drama if it's not necessary."

"What does Ariel want? You must have connected pretty well?"

"Yeah. But that aunt is her mother's sister."

Kate was silent. Ellie didn't blame her. There weren't many encouraging words to say in this situation, except that Ariel might truly benefit more from growing up in Becca Crane's family. She was going to cry again.

"I hope you find a solution that works for all of you," Kate said eventually. "The reason why I'm calling...I was hoping you might be able to join me for a day or two, you and Libby. I miss you—and with everything changing so quickly, I'm scared we're going to lose touch."

"Come on, that's not going to happen..."

"Could you?"

"I'm not sure. There's a lot going on at the moment."

"There's always a lot going on. How did your testimony go?"

"There were a few bumps on the road, but yes. You know, I'll talk to Jordan and Bristol, for different reasons obviously, but I'll see if I can make it happen. I miss you too. Any chance you are going to come back?"

"No."

"What about Derek?"

"What about him?" There was a slight edge to Kate's voice, indicating that this was still a touchy subject.

"I don't know. I thought you might want to work things out. We had some good times hanging out together, didn't we?" This sudden nostalgia obviously came from future plans not working out quite as they had hoped, and Kate didn't share it.

"Yeah, folks on a detective's salary always drinking our beer," she said dryly. "Speaking of which, did you have any other interviews? I hear Homicide is tough to get into."

"True. No, nothing else moved on that front. We wanted to get into the house first, and there was a bit of a rush to it, with Ariel. We even had a room designated to her."

"I'm sorry. Sounds like you could use some old-fashioned girl on girl time—okay...so not what I meant," she added quickly when all Ellie couldn't help laughing at her mistaken metaphor.

"I got you, don't worry," she said, feeling the blood rush to her face at the memory of the previous night. "Okay, maybe if I can narrow down owners of this particular car model some more, I might be able to do a couple of days."

"Please do. We can start planning your housewarming party."

"Sounds good. Talk to you later."

When Ellie ended the call, it occurred to her that Kate had never answered her question about Derek.

Chapter Sixteen

T hey met Dr. Becca Crane the following evening in Mary
Sherman's office. They had spoken briefly to Ariel, who
was moody and withdrawn, as well.

Ellie could sympathize. She had hoped this would get easier,
as long as they were doing the right thing. Learning that Dr.
Crane had indeed hired a lawyer and was seeking to take Ariel
with her by the end of the week, was disconcerting.

"I am sorry it was this hard to find me." She was mid-forties,
a surgeon, returning from a humanitarian mission. Her mother
had never adopted the name of the father Deborah and Becca
had in common, and the sisters had had little contact during
long periods of their lives. "I wanted to stay in touch with Deb,
but let's say, it wasn't easy. She was impulsive, often chasing new
ideas and changing her mind about said ideas and the people
involved." She paused. "I miss her so much." The admission
came out of left field, softening her features.

"I'm sorry for your loss," Ellie said, thinking that Agent
Strickland's assessment of Deborah had sounded different.
Lilah had described her as a mother who would do and risk
anything to remove her daughter from the cult's clutches and
give her a chance at a new life.

"How did you hear about Ariel in the first place?"

"My husband heard the story on the news. Deborah had broken off all contact around the same time she'd met that guy, Nathan, almost fifteen years ago. I did try to find her, but I never could. She'd just vanished, and I wasn't even sure if she..." Dr. Crane swallowed hard. "So here I am, somewhere in the desert with no cell phone reception for months, and the next time I get to a phone, I hear that I have a niece who is at the center of some high-profile trial...I didn't even know about Ariel! I came back as soon as I could."

"Why exactly did Deborah break off the contact?" Ellie asked, well aware she was heading into hazardous waters. However, the woman sitting across from them didn't seem fazed.

"That's a legitimate question, of course. You see, we grew up under very different circumstances. I've been blessed with parents who could open up a wealth of opportunities to me, and I wouldn't be where I am now without them. Deborah, I think, felt like she had to catch up and was failing. I never wanted her to feel this way, but I guess..." She sighed. "I probably didn't make myself clear enough."

Ellie wondered why the father had not extended the same opportunities to his other daughter. She could read the questions in Jordan's face as well.

"You have a daughter," Jordan prompted.

"Yes, Mariah. She's excited to meet Ariel. You can be certain that she'll have a good home with us. It's the least I can do for my sister. I understand that you were supporting her through all this, and I wanted to thank you for it. I was under the impression I'd meet your husband too? Mr. Carpenter?"

An awkward silence ensued.

Jordan cleared her throat. "Detective. Jordan Carpenter. That would be me."

Realization set in, and Ms. Crane quickly schooled her features into a neutral expression. "I see," she said. "I'm really sorry.

I didn't mean to insinuate...anything. It's good to know Ariel would have had someone to take care of her if we hadn't found her, but I'm glad we don't have to worry about that. I hope all the legal aspects will be sorted out in a matter of days. You'll agree that this will be best for Ariel."

Had something in the air changed? Ellie wondered. Maybe she was tired and grasping at straws. It was likely. The doctor had apologized for her assumption.

"Ariel is incredibly smart and savvy, but you have to understand that she has lived for years in a context where everyone, especially women and girls, have been systematically manipulated."

"There was a murderer among them," Ms. Crane said. "Someone didn't take their Commandments too seriously."

"That wasn't all though."

"I understand. I know, there will be challenges, and I can assure you we are well equipped to handle them. I have a request though. Please understand I don't mean to downplay everything you've done for Ariel, both in your job and on a personal level. My husband and I appreciate it so much. Nevertheless, I have to I ask you not to contact her for a while unless it's absolutely necessary for police business. Ariel has been tossed around for some time now. She deserves to be in a stable and permanent home, with her family."

"I'm not sure—" Ellie started, but Jordan stopped her, laying a hand on her arm.

"This is hard for us, too, but we want what's best for Ariel. We will respect your wishes, but we'd like to say goodbye to her."

"Thank you, and of course you can say goodbye. I can give Ariel some of her history. I have pictures from when Deborah and I were younger...and I think this will be important to her, knowing that her mom had a life before that cult."

Ellie wasn't ready to give in yet. "Could I talk to you for a moment?" Those words were directed at Jordan. She was tired and conflicted, but she had to admit Becca Crane did have a point.

"Ellie, let's just do this, okay?"

Dr. Crane smiled uneasily. "Thank you so much for understanding. Ariel is having a hard time now, but with the right guidance, she will thrive."

"I'm sure that's right," Jordan said, and between wanting to snap at her, and forcing herself to take a deep breath, Ellie understood that there was some sort of a plan. Which was good. Ellie was usually the one with the plan, but she hadn't been that good coming up with anything lately.

"I need to speak with Ms. Sherman some more, so you can take a few minutes if she says it's all right. We all have a lot to do now."

⌘

"I have no choice, do I?" Ariel's shoulders were slumped.

"Your aunt wants to concentrate on getting you home as soon as possible," Jordan admitted. "Please remember that everything we said is still true. If you feel uncomfortable at all, let us know."

"How will I do that? Aunt Becca says I'm not supposed to call you or anything. It's going to be a *whole* new chapter in my life."

"With this."

Ellie's jaw dropped when Jordan took a cell phone out of the pocket of her jeans and handed it to Ariel.

"Honey, if you never needed it, that would be the best-case scenario. You don't have to feel obliged to keep in touch with us. But if you ever want to talk, you use this, okay?"

164

Ariel, obviously used to secrets, nodded.

"Thank you. I think that's the first time ever I have a plan B. I appreciate it. Please, look out for the other girls if you can. Not all of them had a mom like I had."

Ellie didn't know what to say—at all. The words she found eventually seemed insufficient, considering the circumstances.

"I think your aunt might need a little time to adjust as well, and when she's a little more comfortable, she might be okay with us talking." Jordan and Ariel looked doubtful, and Ellie wondered if they knew something she didn't.

They heard voices in the hallway, and Ariel jumped to her feet. "Like I said, thank you. I'll let you know how it all works out, and I promise I won't bombard you with texts. Thanks for everything." She hugged them both quickly before the knock on the door preceded Crane and Sherman into the room.

⁂

"I didn't see that one coming," Ellie admitted when they were driving back, on the way to catch up with colleagues at the *Night Shift*. "When did you get that?"

"Lunch break." Jordan looked chastised. "I'm sorry I didn't tell you earlier."

"Wow. We could get in real trouble over this."

"I know, but I don't think that will happen. Ariel's smart. She's not going to let Mrs. 'Where's your husband' catch you."

"You don't know how she meant that. It could have been an honest mistake."

"You saw her face when she realized there was no Mr. Carpenter?"

"Yeah," Ellie admitted, leaning back into the seat with a sigh. "And if we were this wholesome straight couple, she might not have asked us to keep away."

"We're wholesome all right," Jordan said, sounding momentarily amused. "Okay, where were we? If this ever gets out, I'll take the fall—and I don't want you to argue with me on this."

"Fine, I won't, but only because I have something to tell you as well. Kate called...and having the worst timing ever, she asked me to join her for a couple of days. Me and Libby."

"Oh. Weren't we supposed to be painting this weekend?"

"I know, but I guess since Ariel isn't moving in, we could move it up one week?"

"We'll see. Derek already said he'd help. We can do the rest when you're back." Jordan quickly solved the problem.

"Thank you."

Early in the morning, they had breakfast with Libby, who had come to pick up Ellie, and Derek, who had dutifully shown up for the paint job. After the meal, they drove to the house to show Libby around.

"I really wanted to help with that," Ellie said, appropriately chagrined, as they stood by the car.

"Don't feel bad about it." Jordan kissed her. "We'll leave some for you. We are good on the colors, right?"

"Oh yes. No more changes."

"Are you sure? We're not going to do this twice."

"There's no need. Don't get into any trouble while I'm away."

"I'll try not to," Jordan said, amused. "Have fun. I'll see you Monday."

Ellie and Libby got in the car and drove away.

Jordan stayed outside for a moment longer, lost in thought. She hadn't yet processed it all, the good and the bad. She was thrilled that she and Ellie would have their own home—but

Ariel most likely wasn't going to share it with them. She wished she'd asked Ellie to postpone the weekend with Kate. The honking of a car jolted her out of her musings, and she was surprised to see Jack pull up at the curb in his truck.

"Hi, Jack."

He answered the obvious question before she could ask. "If you still want to gut the kitchen, I could help today."

"That's...awesome." Frankly, Jordan hadn't given the specifics much thought.

"The sooner it's done, the sooner you can move in...unless you changed your mind?"

"No. No, we didn't. Thank you."

"Hey Jack. How are the plans for *Carpenter's* going?" Derek, who had come back out, asked, and Jordan shot him a quizzical look. First of all, that name wasn't going to stay, and second, how did he even know about it?

"We ran into each other last week," he explained, aware she had questions. "I think it's a great idea."

Jack smiled. "Thanks. Plans are moving along. How about we get to work then?"

Jordan and Derek went upstairs where they started the task of taping off baseboards and covering the wood floors before getting started with the primer coat. The rooms were fairly square and leveled, so the area was done sooner than they had expected—or maybe it was because they were so carefully avoiding some conversation topics, focusing on the task at hand. The noise from the kitchen downstairs helped as well.

After a lunch break, they went to help Jack while the first coat was still drying, then came back up for the second.

Jordan stood in the doorway of the third bedroom for a moment.

"Please don't say it's the wrong color," Derek commented.

"This was supposed to be Ariel's room." She shook her head. "From the moment we told her, to now, it's still rather surreal. We wanted this so much."

"I'm sorry it didn't work out. Would this be a good moment to ask why I was supposed to do a background check on Rebecca Crane?"

She spun around, all of a sudden guiltily excited. She shouldn't hope for...something to turn things around.

"You got it?"

"You're not answering my question."

"I'd rather not. What does it say?"

"The woman's squeaky clean. Never late paying a bill, gives money to the church, has worked in hospitals all over the world. Can I at least ask what you were hoping to find?"

"Nothing. I hoped you'd find exactly nothing."

Derek didn't look convinced, and Jordan asked herself if she'd told the whole truth. She wanted Ariel to go to a good home, with caring adults. Rebecca Crane and her family seemed to fit that bill, so why did this result leave her with those nagging doubts?

Crane's reaction, if only a minute change of expression, had told volumes.

"I'm not sure I like her," she confessed.

"For any reason other than that she's taking Ariel?" Derek set down the can of paint. "Do you have any suspicion, anything why the girl shouldn't be with her? In that case, now's the time to act. Actually, I'm surprised Ellie is going on a trip now. It's not like you to give in so easily."

"I know! What about the church?"

"Mainstream," Derek said with a shrug. "I don't know the specifics, but it doesn't sound like the Prophets, or any of those "everyone but us goes to hell" folks. Remember it was Deborah who got involved with the cult, not the good doctor."

"Yes, and Deborah recognized her mistake." Jordan raked a hand through her hair. "Crane told us to cut ties with Ariel."

"You're going to do that?"

"I told her yes. And I gave Ariel a phone. Yes, I know this is all a mess, but it freaked me out to think she'd be on her own."

"With family."

Jordan didn't have to say anything for Derek to understand what was on her mind.

"Yeah, sometimes that doesn't mean anything, but from what I understand, she's a far cry from your biological family. Maybe there is something good in this, and after they've all settled in, she won't be so opposed to your checking in on Ariel."

"Ellie said the same thing."

"Yeah, well, trust your woman. We're going to finish this room or not?"

"I guess. Let's get going."

Chapter Seventeen

K ate had a cozy apartment upstairs in her grandparents' house, complete with a balcony and a guest room big enough for twin beds. After she had introduced everybody, and Libby and Ellie had time to freshen up, they left for the restaurant where Kate had reserved a table.

"How are you doing?" Ellie finally asked.

"Frankly? I'm great for the most part. I have stayed away from the news best I could, though I did hear about the trial. Those poor women."

Kate looked better than she had in a long time, Ellie had to admit, though she wasn't sure if helping out in the grandparents' hardware store was all she'd ever want to do. Maybe that was just her. Whatever the job had thrown at her, she couldn't imagine doing anything else, but their situations differed greatly. Ellie had found love. The same job had made Kate a widow before she had a chance to say yes. The thought made her shudder.

"We hope all of the men, and some of the women will serve prison sentences," she said. "After all they knew about the underage marriages, if not the serial killer under their roof. But, let's talk about something else."

"Yes. How's it going with Ariel?" Libby asked.

There hadn't been much time to update all of their friends on the latest developments.

"Not good, I'm afraid. An aunt of hers came forward, and she's going to live with her."

They had the first bottle of wine on the table, a context that seemed too nice and bubbly to catch her friends up on the newest development.

For a moment, both Libby and Kate were silent.

"I'm sorry," Libby mumbled. "I didn't mean to—"

"No, come on, it's not your fault."

"Perhaps there's a silver lining in that."

Kate's statement put Ellie on the defensive.

"Why do you say that? We both have steady incomes, and we just bought a house. We even showed her a room that would be hers. What makes you think that we wouldn't be able to take care of her?"

"Ellie, slow down. I can hardly judge anyone on their life choices right now. I was just thinking...with the house, and the new job you're going to get sometime soon, it would be a lot. Sure, she's a teenager, that's not like having a baby, but she had to deal with a lot of crap. You guys aren't really home that much."

It was an uncomfortable thought.

"I know...but she was so brave, and she had no one. We would have made it work. We still will if the aunt doesn't work out."

"What makes you think that?" Libby asked.

"I don't know, the fact that she's a surgeon who flies around the world to help poor people, or the nice house she and her husband have?" Ellie sighed. "Yeah, right. I think I need a refill."

"You guys are going to be all right, and so is she." Kate patted her shoulder.

"I know. So, what are you going to do about Derek? It's really over with you two?"

"Okay, I guess that's a fair question. I don't want to come back to the job, but I might move back to town at some point. I don't know yet, but we didn't have much of a chance to talk, and...I'll give him that if he's still interested."

"I think that's a good idea."

Ellie was wondering if, at home, Jordan was having the same thoughts. There was nothing left they could do other than hope that Ariel would be happy with her new-found family. Because they'd promised her that she mattered most.

❧

That nagging uncomfortable feeling didn't go away, not even after she'd had a brief conversation with Ellie on the phone. It intensified when she and Derek went for a beer at the end of the day, and Marcus Holmes was once again sitting at the bar.

"You want me to talk to him?" Derek asked, and Jordan gave him a wry smile in return.

"I'll be right back."

She was aware that Holmes had watched her, though he turned to the bartender only seconds before she had reached the counter.

"Detective Carpenter," he said without looking at her. "We meet again." There was a smile in his voice.

"Why do you keep coming to this place?"

He shrugged. "I like it. Good drinks, food...company sometimes. I actually enjoy talking to you."

Sadly, she couldn't tell him to stay away from the *Night Shift* without good reason. Perhaps she should have redirected her focus from Becca Crane to the man showing up in places that she frequented...She wasn't ready to let her off the hook though. Jordan trusted Ariel to let them know if anything was wrong. As for Holmes...

"I hoped you'd be here tonight," he said.

"Really."

"Jonathan Darby died earlier today, some complications, I heard. You probably know already...Oh. You didn't," he said, having caught her minute reaction of...what? Relief? Jordan wasn't sure, but it must have shown in her face. "All the more reasons for us to connect. I guess you could say we both got into real trouble because of him."

"I don't need to connect," Jordan mumbled. "How did you find out?"

"Donovan. He works with my lawyer as well, so he knew I had...an interest in the story."

"Lovely. Enjoy your drink."

"What happened?" Derek asked when she returned to the table, handed him his beer and took a swig of hers. Across the room, Holmes took a bill out of his wallet that he tossed onto the counter and left.

"Apparently...Darby is dead. I guess it's still under tabs, but Holmes' lawyer works with Donovan, so he got the news exclusively. Couldn't wait to tell me."

"And?"

Jordan sighed. "Hell if I know. For sure, I'm not sad to hear this. I don't feel like dancing on his grave either. It's just...nothing."

"You've had a lot on your plate lately."

"Well, yeah, everyone has. To victory over evil...I guess."

Their bottles clinked together. Jordan wondered what Ellie was doing at this moment, wishing she'd be waiting for her at home.

It turned out they had both dreaded going back to an empty apartment, which was mostly the reason why they walked the few blocks down the road to Derek's apartment, making a stop at the liquor store on the way. Meanwhile, the news about the serial killer passing away in prison had broken. Making a grimace, Derek turned off the TV.

"They give a lot of fame and attention to the bad guys. He'd love that."

"Oh yes. But he's not loving anything anymore. Let's talk about something nicer. When are you going to call Kate?"

Derek gave her a quizzical look. "She called it quits. Why would I do that?"

"You miss her."

"Wow, Harding's a terrible influence. Nine years with a shrink, and you've never been this chatty."

"Funny." It probably wasn't Ellie's influence, but the number of beers they'd had that made the difference at the moment. "You know it's true."

"Can we go back to the serial killer?"

"No," she said, making a non-committal sound. "I have no desire to ever go back there."

"Sorry. Yes, I miss her. Are you happy now?"

Jordan leaned back on the couch, pondering that question. She certainly had hoped for a different outcome on some things—the adoption, and her other plan for which the timing never seemed right.

"Yes. I am. We'll keep tabs on Dr. Crane for now, make sure she's everything we hope she is. I want to marry Ellie. The sooner the better."

"That's great. Why are you telling me first?"

"Wait, what makes you think I haven't told her yet?"

Derek surveyed the bottles on the table, looking back at her. His gaze spoke volumes.

"Yeah, you can see I haven't changed all that much. It's not that it's a big decision. I'm good with big decisions. There was just no time to do it right."

"If you say so."

As the night went on, Jordan accepted Derek's offer to crash on his couch—she hadn't been looking forward to moving far from it anyway. The questions kept her up, though, and they seemed to get more urgent by the minute. There were several people whose opinion she could have asked, but not at this time of night. It was worth a shot. She knocked on his bedroom door and went inside.

Derek didn't even look surprised. She took that as an invitation to sit on the other side of the bed and begin.

"It's about Kathryn. Jim, too, but mostly her."

"You're not sure whether to invite them?"

"That's not it, but I think she expects it. There are other people who really made an effort. It wouldn't be fair to them."

"You mean your parents. Do you really think they'd mind if Kathryn was there? Have you asked them?"

"That's your answer for everything," Jordan complained, idly wondering at how many beers they'd stopped earlier. She still felt slightly dizzy—or maybe it was the subject. "You'll be invited. Kate will be there for sure."

"Relax. We're not going to cause a scene at your wedding. You'll be fine."

"Thank you," she said, hiding a yawn behind her hand.

"No, I mean, you'll be fine. With everything. It will be even better now that one problem, by which I mean Darby, solved itself. As for the other subject, I know it's tough right now, but if you want children, there are always other ways."

Jordan had several thoughts on that, and she was grateful for him listening to her ramblings in the middle of the night, but the context struck her as highly amusing.

"That's not what I meant, and you know it." He couldn't help laughing either. "Have you even bought a ring?"

"I'll pick it up tomorrow."

"Yep, that's what I thought."

❧

Ellie and Libby had driven back early on Monday morning, going directly to work. Ellie hadn't seen Jordan yet, but sitting at her desk, she was pleased to make more progress on the list of red Volvos. She was down to five owners, one of which had a record, including vandalism and B&E. Going over the names, Ellie was startled to find a familiar one: Lillian Bishop. A quick search revealed that Lillian was the mother of Jeffrey Bishop who had been Colin Buck's roommate, and a member in the online serial killer fan club.

Certainly, Jordan and Derek would be interested in asking him about meeting the photographer, Paul Burton. She was about to call when Sergeant Bristol came out of his office, heading straight for her desk.

"Harding, I just got a call from Lieutenant Carroll," he said. "He'd like to see you in his office."

"Of course. Is everything all right? Did he say what it's about?"

"He will tell you."

Ellie's heart started beating faster. This could be about a simple assignment, but then again, nearly everyone in the department knew about her and Jordan's relationship, including Jordan's boss. What did he have to say to her that he couldn't say in public? She had just received a text from Jordan this morning, so this could have nothing to do with her?

She hasted upstairs, catching her breath before she knocked on Carroll's door.

"Officer Harding, come on in."

Once they were seated, the lieutenant wasted no time.

"Detective Waters has given me notice that he wants to retire by the end of the year," he said.

"Oh my God." Ellie cleared her throat when she got a quizzical look in reaction. "I mean...I thought this was about...I'm sorry." Her relief aside, she didn't like this situation at all. Coming straight to work from the all-girls weekend, getting flustered because of a misunderstanding, this wasn't how she wanted to present herself to her future boss.

"It would be best to find a replacement while he's still here. I hear you might be interested in the position."

"Yes, sir, I am."

Ellie's heart was still pounding, for a completely different reason now.

"Good. I wanted to give you a heads-up on this. You've worked well with my detectives before..." She hoped she wasn't blushing too hard. Work wasn't all she'd done with one of his detectives. "...so I expect this to work out. You'll be notified of the date for your interview."

"Thank you, sir. I really appreciate it."

They shook hands, and Ellie left the lieutenant's office with excitement, and a tinge of guilt creeping in, for being this happy when Ariel's situation was still somewhat up in the air. Ellie hoped that the girl would find a loving, supportive home with the Cranes. They had to push their own hopes for the future aside for this.

"Ellie, hi."

"Derek. Thanks again for helping out with the painting. I haven't seen the house or Jordan today, though..." It occurred to her that having spent the weekend with the woman who had just broken up with him, made the situation slightly awkward. "Um...I think I have something for you. Remember Jeffrey Bishop? The owner of the dark red Volvo, that's his mother. It seems like there is a connection between the break-in and Darby's fan club."

"Good job. I'm going to see him right now. Why don't you come with me?"

Great. More opportunity for awkward conversations. Kate had indicated that she wasn't entirely happy with her decision, but Ellie had promised not to tell anyone.

"Sure. Jordan isn't here?"

"She was going to check out something else, but she said you could check the progress on the house during lunch break."

"Sounds good. I swear I'm not going to bail on any more weekends...Lieutenant Carroll told me Waters is going to retire. I'll still have to go through the process, but he seems to think I'm a good candidate for the job."

Ellie had wanted to wait to tell Jordan first, but she couldn't seem to hold it in any longer. She had waited so long for this moment to arrive.

"If he calls you here to tell you about it, that means something. That's great, congratulations."

"Thank you. You're the first to know," she said, baffled when Derek rolled his eyes and said, "You guys. You should really talk to each other once in a while."

Chapter Eighteen

After breakfast at Derek's, where they had both spoken to each other in quiet tones, for a good reason, Jordan had spent Sunday cleaning up in the house before she picked up the ring. Lunch break on Monday might give her time enough...

She received Ellie's text regarding the owner of the Volvo when she was a block away from campus. She was almost there when she saw Bishop get into a van and drive away. Jordan followed him down various streets to the harbor, and then further into the industrial district. When he parked, she did too at a distance and called Derek back.

"Looks like he's waiting for someone. How about you join the party? This could be interesting."

"Don't say that word. I still have a headache."

"Right. This will be the last time I'll ever wake up in your bed. Let's never speak of it again."

"Um, Ellie's here," he said, chuckling, and she realized he'd put her on speaker.

"Guys?" she heard Ellie's voice. "I feel like there's something you should explain to me."

"Don't worry, it was harmless. Speaking of the weekend, will you have time around noon to go take a look at the fruits of our labor?"

"Sure. I'd still like to know..."

"I'll leave Derek to explain that to you," Jordan said, laughing. "I should get a little closer. I'll see you in a bit."

She got out of her car and walked closer to the vehicle Bishop had driven here before he vanished into the building. Jordan wondered if they'd finally find the clues as to who had broken into Lori Gleason's house.

"We drank, we talked, we fell asleep. I swear there's nothing you need to be worried about."

Derek had misinterpreted Ellie's silence. "I'm not worried," she said, still trying to get hold of what was nagging at the back of her mind. "Come on. I was just thinking..." There was something that seemed familiar, something she couldn't put her finger on. After days of trying to narrow down the type of car, Bishop showed up in this van, in this area...In her mind, she went through the previous cases they had worked together, connections, until it came to her.

She'd been here before. Sheila Irwin's ex had hired a couple of goons to rob and vandalize her sex shop—he had rented an office in this area. The main perpetrator, a man by the name of Randy Wheeler, going by HotStud69 online, had denied vandalizing Jordan's front door as well.

"Is it paranoid to think that the same folks who wrote 'bitch' on Jordan's front door, could be part of Darby's fan club?" she wondered out loud.

"Aren't they behind bars now?"

"Not all of them. I think at least one of Randy's buddies got probation, and the ex-husband...I'm not sure."

"It's a theory," Derek ascertained. "Excuse me," he added when his cell phone rang. It was still on speaker, so Ellie could hear Jordan talk.

"This is interesting. Are you anywhere nearby now?"

"Ten minutes max," Derek said.

"Good. I think I found something..."

The line went dead.

❦

The hit wasn't strong enough to knock her out, but she still ended up face first on the concrete, her gun skidding out of reach. Relying on strength rather than skill, the attacker tried to drag her behind the metal doors and inside.

"Please, stop it," a familiar voice said. "We've come so close. You don't think this was all going away, didn't you?"

The man let go of her, and Jordan immediately understood why. Jeffrey Bishop had a gun trained on her.

"It's okay, I can take care of this," he said. The other man, apparently another buddy from the serial killer fan club, nodded and turned to walk away. "Now, go inside, please."

"This is not going to work." Jordan cast a glance at the display to her left, barely suppressing a shudder. "My colleagues are on their way."

"No, they're not. You still have nothing...and now that our mutual friend is dead, there is no witness connecting us. And there won't be. Now go. I want you to see what we prepared for you."

"Jeffrey, don't be stupid."

"No, you don't be stupid. I could hurt you with this."

He raised the gun a few inches. Unfortunately, he was right about that. Backup would be here any minute, so she had to stall best she could.

This time, the admirers hadn't gone with a live model. The mannequin's wrists were tied together above her head, the chain attached to a hook in the ceiling. She couldn't look, couldn't get distracted—or remember, though she couldn't suppress the gasp.

"What do you want with all this anyway? You really think you can scare Lori Gleason—or me—after everything?"

His finger was still on the trigger, though relaxed. He and Holmes were wannabes, admirers of a killer. If she could keep him talking, get him to let his guard down…This time, it wasn't her tied up. In fact, there was so much clutter behind her it gave her options.

"It's not about what happened. It's about finishing it. What do you think? We had Colin ask the details. He hated it, but he did. That's why Darby wrote you the letter. To tell you about what's coming." He glanced quickly over to the mannequin. There was a red line on the doll's thigh, like blood from a cut. The disgusting display had been created with a love for detail.

"He did. And he instructed you. I guess there were some things he neglected to mention."

Bishop howled and let go of the gun when the metal pipe hit him. Clutching his side, he scrambled for it, but Jordan got there first.

"It ends here," she said. "It's finished."

There were voices at the door, and a moment later Derek appeared, with the other man in cuffs. Ellie came running inside to put the cuffs on Bishop as well, while he was complaining loudly.

"Jordan, are you okay?"

She stopped cold at the sight of the mannequin.

"Sick." Derek sounded disgusted.

"Yeah. We need to pick up Marcus Holmes as well and…" She winced, and a split-second later, Ellie was by her side.

"You're bleeding," she said. "Let's take care of this first. I have a few ideas about who else might be part of this club."

Fortunately, the unpleasant encounter hadn't led to more than a cut on her temple and a few bruises. Jordan didn't want to go home—cleaning up the last of the messes Darby had created, seemed like a much better solution, and it would keep her occupied.

The warehouse turned out to be a cornucopia of evidence, from the equipment that had been used for the photograph left at Lori's, to the spray paint used to write a slur on her front door months ago. This was how long they'd been planning this, with Colin, with Jonathan Darby who had hoped to live the fulfillment of his fantasies vicariously.

All of it was going to fall apart, and she didn't want to miss a moment of it.

Walking past the interrogation rooms, Jordan noticed Marcus Holmes in one of them, already talking to Donovan.

"What happened to his other lawyer?"

"He didn't give an explanation, just said that Donovan would handle the case."

"Interesting," she said to the lieutenant who was also watching from the other side of the glass. "I can see why Donovan would want to do it. This is right up his alley."

"Shouldn't you be home?"

She laughed wryly. "I'm not even sure where home is at the moment. But no, I'm fine. And something about Donovan doesn't sit right with me. He always denied that he let Colin Buck talk to Darby, but these guys claim Colin got all the details of his crimes out of him? Bishop says that's why Darby wrote the letter. He couldn't have done it without help. I'm not sure what to believe."

"Either way, it's over."

"You don't have to tell me that. I know. I want to talk to Holmes."

"I'll be right outside," Carroll said.

Jordan walked inside only to have Donovan jump to his feet. He looked outraged.

"What are you holding my client for? He has nothing to do with whatever happened this afternoon!"

"We are going over Mr. Bishop's phone records right now, and there were plenty of prints at the warehouse. I believe there's a good reason for Mr. Holmes to be here."

"Oh, come on, Detective," Holmes said. "You know I'm interested in these things, in theory. Did we ask Colin to talk to Mr. Darby, yes."

"Marcus, I'd advise you to be silent."

"What's the harm? The detective already knows that we used to talk about Mr. Darby a lot. Does it make us a bit odd? Sure. That's not the same as planning a murder, right, Detective?"

"Unless you did indeed plan a murder. What was the final goal in all of this? To discuss murder in theory over a few beers, or to figure out how to get away with it? Mr. Darby certainly had the idea you might continue his legacy."

"With all due respect, that's ridiculous."

"You knew about Darby's death before it was in the press."

"He was my client," Donovan told her. "Of course I would be informed...and when Mr. Holmes asked me about it, I saw no reason not to tell, seeing that the story would break within a few hours."

"Marcus, have you ever been to the warehouse? Your interest went as far as recreating Darby's crime scenes?"

"That's outrageous. We're leaving right now—"

"I don't believe you will."

Behind the lieutenant, Casey and A.D.A. Esposito came inside.

"What is this—"

"You're under arrest for conspiring to murder Colin Buck," Carroll said to Donovan. "For starters."

Valerie stayed in the room after Carroll, Casey, and a loudly protesting Donovan were gone.

"It's time we talk for real, Marcus," she said. "If Jeffrey talks first, it won't look good for you, and besides, I think you both want to give up the person who made your club possible in the first place."

"I wanted to know," he said. "It was like a movie, okay? I wanted to know what it felt like, but I didn't think we were going to murder anyone."

"What about finishing what Darby started?" Jordan asked, feeling her stomach churn. "You didn't sign up for that either?"

He looked up at her, holding her gaze for a long moment. Then he smiled.

"Words will do, Marcus," Jordan reminded him after a tense moment of silence, in which she suppressed a shudder. If he had practiced that expression in the mirror, he couldn't have come closer to his idol. "Colin, obviously, was the pawn in that game. What about your buddies who pretended to film a horror movie? Did they know it was more than that? Who else?"

Holmes was still far too comfortable. "Mr. Darby was by far the most interesting individual we could find, so of course he was the king. He told Colin that you were his all time favorite, so I guess that makes you queen."

All it made her at the moment was nauseated, wishing she could get up and leave. But someone had to see this through, and she didn't want to show him any weakness.

"Whether or not he told Colin anything, we'll probably never know. But he warned me. I think he was a little fed up with amateurs trying to take his place."

"We're no amateurs!"

Gone was the smile and the conversational tone, and this time, Jordan flinched, because the behavioral patterns were so reminiscent. A wannabe, maybe, but he had done his homework.

"I believe you. Go on," Valerie said. "I'm interested in your side of the story."

...so it would finally be over.

Chapter Nineteen

I n the afternoon, Ellie came to take her to the break room for a quick, improvised meal. Even though the images still running through her head were sickening, Jordan found to her surprise that she was actually hungry.

"Where did you get soup?" she wondered out loud.

"I stopped at the deli down the street. I know neither of us is going home early."

"Probably not," Jordan agreed, and with a sigh, Ellie sank into the bench next to her, leaning close.

Jordan didn't have to ask. She was freaked out enough as it was about the sparsely clothed mannequin tied up with chains. Okay, it would be better to push that image out of her mind for a bit. Otherwise, she wouldn't be able to eat.

"I'm so glad you're okay," Ellie whispered. "We heard...on the phone."

"Yeah, not the highlight of my day. But it was a good thing you remembered Wheeler and the vandalism case. We got them all, and even Donovan will have a lot to answer for."

"That's good." Ellie straightened. "We'll have to talk about Ariel, right? I mean...Some more."

"Yes. And we will."

Ariel hadn't used the phone, most likely, because she understood about emergencies, and none had happened yet.

"Let's talk to Dr. Crane again. She might change her mind on us checking in on Ariel once she's all settled in." She took a spoonful of the soup. "You have no idea how much I love you right now."

If this was out of context, she was lucky that Ellie understood anyway.

"Anytime. I'm afraid I have to go, but we could stop by the house tonight...and check when we can have the movers?"

"That would be nice. Thank you. I'll see you later."

Ellie kissed her, waved and left.

As Jordan finished her meal, she was going over the subjects they needed to address in the immediate future. Movers. In the chaos of the day, she had forgotten to tell Ellie they'd have to put in the new kitchen first.

She had put most of her own furniture in storage after selling her house, not that there was a lot. She had bought it furnished, and there had never been enough time to add many pieces. They would have to make some purchases. She believed the couch at Ellie and Kate's belonged to Kate.

There was a lot to do.

Ariel wouldn't move in with them.

Jordan still had to ask Ellie the all-important question, and it was important to do it at the right time.

❧

She almost went back to the break room when she saw Rebecca Crane sitting in the visitor's chair at her desk. A bit of paperwork, make sure she had all the information on today's bust—that had been the plan.

Jordan made the more mature choice, but barely. The food, while welcome, hadn't made the headache go away.

"Ms. Crane. How can I help you?"

In an instant, she was struggling with a kaleidoscope of mixed emotions. She wanted Ariel to be well, to be in a good family. But if Rebecca Crane came to see her here, after declaring they shouldn't contact Ariel, what did that mean?

Jordan hoped she hadn't found the phone. Not today, she couldn't deal with this.

"Detective, I was hoping I could talk to you." She sounded serene, but not exactly disturbed.

"Is Ariel okay?" Jordan took a seat across from the woman who openly studied her.

"Yes, she is. That looks like you had a rough day."

"I've had worse. Why are you here, then?" She took a deep breath, aware of the edge to her voice. "I'm sorry. You were right about the day, but that's no reason to take it out on you."

Ms. Crane laughed ruefully. "Oh, I understand that you're not thrilled to see me. I just think that the last time we met, a few things were left unsaid...and maybe I said too much. I was so excited to find Ariel, trying to deal with my grief at the same time, and...I guess I didn't deal so well with the fact that she already had someone looking after her. Someone who'd be more than capable."

"You're family."

"Yes. I'm lucky I have that going for me. And you'll never know how grateful I am that you were ready to become hers in case something had gone wrong."

Jordan restrained herself, from getting emotional, from wanting to present the many good reasons she and Ellie had for wanting to help Ariel.

"But it didn't."

"No, thank God. So much has gone wrong already, Deb, everything she and Ariel went through. I know you saw some of that up close. I had a talk with my niece, and I told her she could keep the phone."

"Oh. That's kind of you. I actually don't have any excuse for this."

"Deb and I didn't always have the best of relationships. I'm aware I have a lot to make up for myself, but I'm willing to do that, and meanwhile...I want Ariel to trust me. I want her to understand I'm not going to leave her behind."

"That's good. She needs that stability right now."

"I agree. I...I overreacted, and I'm sorry about that. Ariel connected with you both, I realize, and you are welcome to visit her. Convince yourself that she's going to be all right."

Slowly but surely the day was beginning to take its toll. Jordan realized there might be a limit as to how many emotional subjects she'd be able to handle tonight. "Thank you. I'm grateful you're not reporting me. I did cross a line." She hoped the conversation wouldn't go on much longer.

"We all want what's best for Ariel."

"Yes, we do. You were quite surprised to realize there was no husband." If they were having this heart to heart, Jordan might get that answer as well.

"Believe me, that was not my concern. I love my niece, and she felt safe enough with you to want to be a family. Once that sank in, I couldn't possibly keep you out of her life. I have to go now, but why don't you two come for dinner soon? I could call you."

"Yes, thank you."

They both got to her feet, and Jordan shook hands with Ariel's aunt.

Afterwards she texted Ellie.

"I'm ready to call it a day. What about you?"

"I can't, yet," came the answer within minutes. "I'll try to be home in an hour or so?"

All of a sudden, Jordan had an idea about what to do in that hour.

❦

Rebecca Crane's background check had come clean. The church she was involved in did not engage in blatant homophobia, and she and her husband did have the perfect means to care for Ariel. That made it a little easier.

Still, it was with a heavy heart that Jordan pulled up at Jack and Pauline's house. It was curious that while living with Bethany, she hardly ever made an unannounced visit. Mostly, she didn't know what to talk about. She'd felt there was nothing much she could tell them about her day-to-day life, the smaller or bigger arguments, and her own growing worry that this might be all.

Ellie had brought so many new options into her life Jordan hadn't even considered before. Marriage...Becoming parents. The latter was not something that would happen so soon.

Ariel would be fine.

She and Ellie would be fine. Eventually.

Pauline could have probably read in her face that today hadn't gone all that well, if the Band-Aid hadn't been a dead giveaway.

"Jordan! Are you all right? Is Ellie?"

"Yes, everything's fine. Ellie is still at work."

"Come on in. What happened?"

"Most of the men from the cult were convicted, everything from reckless child endangerment to assault."

"That's a good thing, right?" Pauline sounded surprised for a reason. Jordan could count on one hand the number of occasions she had brought shop talk to her parents.

"Yes, absolutely. We had a good case. And...It turns out that Ariel has living blood relatives after all," Jordan told her as she took off her coat. "An aunt of hers, her mother's sister, came forward."

Pauline's arms were around her the next moment, as she understood, more than almost anyone else, what that meant.

"Oh honey, I don't know what to say. It's a good thing for her, but...I know."

It didn't take long for Jordan to be slightly uncomfortable, so when she stepped away and wiped her face, Pauline didn't try to stop her.

"I'm so sorry," she said instead. "I know how much you'd hoped this could happen. Will you be able to keep in touch?"

"I think so. They live in the next town."

"Okay. And there's this other plan you have...that one is still on the table, right?"

"Of course. It's been for a while." Jordan finally followed her into the living room.

"I'm glad to hear that. We really look forward to planning this with you two. Would you like to stay for dinner so we can talk about it?"

"Oh, no. Ellie doesn't know yet."

Pauline smiled. "I wouldn't be so sure, but you're right, you should talk to her. And I'm sorry for all the hints I gave you about kids. You do it when the time is right, and you'll be great. This time...it wasn't right."

"I guess not. I better go. Ellie will be home soon, and we have to finalize some details about the move."

"This is an exciting time. Try to enjoy it. It doesn't mean you're letting Ariel down, on the contrary."

Jordan's doubts must have shown in her face, because she added, "Don't go there. You were always responsible, and that's why you're doing what's right. Kathryn had to learn a lot, and she needed a long time to get there, not that it's up to me to judge. This is what I can see: You're not like her. That's just a fact."

"Thank you, Mom." This time, Jordan initiated the hug. She couldn't wait to get home.

⁓

"So, Wheeler, Donovan, Holmes and Bishop where all part of the club," Ellie surmised as they sat over take-out, looking at couches online. "What a bunch of losers."

She had tried to get through the day best she could, and knowing Jordan had spent the afternoon safe at the department, had helped—but the display at the warehouse had rattled her.

They had both done their best to move past the serial killer's basement and everything that had happened there. Men like Holmes and his group were a special kind of evil.

"That sums it up nicely," Jordan said. "So—what about this couch?" The light grey would fit well with the wall colors."

"It's small."

"It's big enough for two people, don't you think?"

"Today really sucked. I don't know any other way to say it." Ellie was well aware that her words presented a non-sequitur, but she also knew that the two of them were good at postponing necessary conversations. Right now, though, there was so much happening in their lives that simply couldn't wait.

Jordan leaned against the back of the couch—Kate's, which was why they couldn't take it with them—studying her with amusement. "Where are you going with this?"

"There is so much going on. I didn't even have the chance to tell you that Carroll asked me into his office today. Waters is retiring and I should interview for the job—"

"What? That is amazing! Congratulations!"

"Yes. Thanks. I don't have the job yet, but it's great." Ellie jumped to her feet. "I'm really happy about it, but I also realize we've been taking on a lot. And we would have tried to make it work, but maybe, for some things, we weren't ready."

"I know. Please, sit back down. That is part of what I wanted to talk to you about. When Ms. Crane came to the station earlier, she apologized, and she said we could see Ariel. We had a good talk even though...It hurt."

Ellie could feel that hurt echoing within herself. All her life, she had dealt with roadblocks one way: Head on. Her career plans were working out after a small delay, but she'd never expected having to admit there was something she couldn't do, at least not now.

"I understand. We would have done our best, right? And maybe, now that it's not going to happen, we have to learn something from this. Start our life together. Just be together for a while."

"That sounds good to me. I still think the couch is fine."

"Let's forget about the couch for a moment. I...There is something else I need to tell you. Actually...ask."

She felt dizzy for a short moment, wondering if that was a normal reaction. There was one thing Ellie knew for sure—it was now or never, regardless of everything else they were dealing with at this moment, this was the right time. She stepped out of her heels, got down on one knee and took the ring out of the pocket of her skirt.

She hadn't spent all evening at work but instead used some of the time to pick up the ring she'd chosen.

Jordan looked startled, her eyes welling up at the sight. Or maybe Ellie was imagining the latter because her own vision had become blurry.

"I know we have had a tendency to rush into things—well, I have. But we both agreed that we would be the best family we could be for Ariel, we just didn't know that something better was going to come along for her. I know you're sad. I am too, but this is the right thing to do. Regardless of everything else, I want to be with you, wake up with you every day, and I didn't mean to go off on a tangent. Please marry me?"

"Of course. Yes, I will marry you." Jordan pulled her up and into her arms for wordless affirmation. It wasn't until several minutes later that she admitted, "You were braver than I was. I did buy a ring...and then I was waiting for the right moment."

"What did you think was going to happen? You didn't think I'd say no?"

"No. No, I guess not." Jordan laughed self-consciously. "Okay, let's move on."

"Sure. It's all right. You'll have the first then."

"The first what?"

"Baby, of course." Ellie started laughing at Jordan's perplexed expression. "I'm kidding. Come on, I want to see my ring too."

Jordan had barely put it on her finger when her cell phone rang.

"It's Ariel," she said, her tone somber. As soon as she read the text message, a smile lit up her face, and Ellie could breathe again. Jordan held the screen out to her.

Sorry, this is not an emergency! You probably know by now that we got busted, but Becca is cool with the phone. She said to ask if you wanted to come by for dinner on Sunday.

"This is good news," Ellie said even though the room was starting to blur again.

"It is. We say yes, right?"

"Yes, we do."

Jordan answered the message, and they abandoned the search for the perfect couch in favor of celebrating the future, and, because it mattered, mourning what they couldn't have—not yet.

It wasn't until much later that Ellie remembered to tease Jordan some more about the night at Derek's.

"Really, you're still worried about that?" Jordan asked, amused. "We talked. He thought I should get my act together and ask you to marry me. That worked out. I think he should call Kate, but that's none of our business."

"Speaking of which…" Not telling Derek was one thing, but Ellie wasn't going to have secrets from her wife-to-be.

"She is thinking about coming back, so they can talk it out. You think they can make it work?"

"They better. They'll have a wedding to attend soon," Jordan said and pulled her close again.

Jordan dreamed about the trailer that night, the time, one of the times, she'd been looking for her parents and couldn't find them. The door wasn't locked, so she held on to the stuffed teddy bear and continued her search outside. The next-door neighbors had a loud argument that had kept her from sleeping all night. A woman was crying.

She was scared.

Obviously, that moment, Kathryn had been scared too, because when they found her almost wandering off into the near-by forest, her eyes were red-rimmed.

"What the hell do you think you're doing?"

The bitter reproach stung more than the slap itself.

Fast forward to a conversation with Bethany she'd regret for a long time to come—because she'd been drunk and scared, and for the life of her, she couldn't find a reason to carry on with this. Bethany, of course, specialized in difficult cases, and she had her own issues as well.

"You wouldn't do anything like that. You wouldn't do that to me, right?" Jordan knew she had spooked herself already enough to walk away from the precipice, but that line had been thin, and Bethany had been there, reason enough to feel indebted to her for years to come.

Trapped.

She startled herself awake before her mind could take the nightmare any further. She wasn't trapped any longer.

Instead, she was going to marry the woman she loved and build a home with her. Jordan scooted closer to lay an arm around Ellie's waist.

Life was good.

About the Author

B arbara Winkes writes sapphic crime drama and Christ-
mas romance. She loves writing characters who get the
job done, whether it's stopping a predator or saving cherished
traditions—while still making time for love. She lives with her
wife in Quebec City.

barbarawinkes.com

Also by Barbara Winkes

The Crossing Lines Trilogy
Undercover
Redemption
Vengeance

The Connected Series
Promised to the Queen
Drawn to the Enemy
Tempted by the Protector

Kelli & Merin Romantic Suspense
Thunder
Rain

Standalone
The Amnesia Project